ICE QUEEN

Teenage Survivalist III

Julie L. Casey

Amazing Things Press

Book design by Julie L. Casey

ISBN 978-1945667565

Printed in the United States of America.

For more information, visit

www.teenagesurvivalist.com
or
www.amazingthingspress.com

For Vona,

the smartest, sweetest person I know,
whose stories of her life and pets,
especially a Weimeraner named Spook,
have enthralled me for years.

I love you and miss you.
You will always be in my heart.

Chapter 1
Unicorns and Ice

Dad charged into my room madder than a sow separated from her piglets. He was yelling that I was holding out on him, that I had some dope hidden somewhere in my room. I froze, holding my glass unicorn and looking down at the floor to avoid a confrontation. That seemed to make him even angrier, and he slapped my hand, sending the unicorn flying across the room where it struck my desk and landed on the floor, its horn broken off. I just stared at it, refusing to let my anguish show to the man who had simultaneously saved me and made my entire life miserable.

"Ice Queen," he sneered. He always called me that. At least it was better than the nickname he used to call me when I was a little girl—*Tattle Taylor*. I was angry with him, an emotion that felt as familiar to me as my own name, but I also felt sorry for him. I know that seems unfathomable for someone who has never lived like this, but I knew he couldn't help it. I knew he was hurting, that the demons in his mind had come calling again. But this time there were no drugs, prescribed or otherwise, to help calm their strident demands. I feared that in time, without some substance to keep the demons at bay, he would get worse, the demons taking over his mind, his humanity. So I tried to stay calm, non-confrontational as always, to be as quiet and insignificant in his life as possible, so as not to incite the demons to action.

Dad had never been diagnosed with a particular mental illness, but everyone who knew him well could tell there was something not right about him. He never talked about the voices to anyone except Mom, preferring to self-medicate with marijuana at first, then crack cocaine, heroine, and meth. And always alcohol, of course. I often overheard him talking to her at night when my bedroom next to theirs.

"Libby," I'd hear him say, sobbing. "I'm scared they'll make me do something I don't want to do."

"Just hold on a little longer, Kyle," she'd answer, half soothingly, half distracted. "We'll find some ice for you soon."

"Ice" was how they referred to their current drug of choice, the latest having been crystal meth. Mom was ill equipped to help him, though. She struggled from her own problems—depression, I suppose—which made her crave the diversion of drugs and alcohol almost as much as Dad did.

Dad picked up the broken unicorn and stood looking at it for a moment. In that short span of time, the madness seemed to ebb out of him, his body slowly deflating like a balloon that had a pinprick hole in it. When he looked up at me, I could see sadness and remorse in his eyes. Maybe even a plea for forgiveness. He held the diminished figurine out to me and I looked away as I took it from him, not wanting to antagonize him into anger again nor wanting to forgive his behavior yet, even though I knew in my heart I always would. He turned away and left the room, closing the door quietly behind him. I finally released the tears as I stared at the once magical creature that had now been reduced to a mere ordinary horse with a bump on its head.

The precious memories came flooding into my mind—my grandmother taking me at the age of nine to see *The Glass Menagerie* on stage. I was enchanted by the crystal animals and drawn to the character of Laura, who preferred to stay home with her menagerie rather than venture out into the world. I understood how she felt. The times I lived with my Grammy, when Mom and Dad were in rehab or jail or just on one of their binges, I never wanted to leave. I felt safe and unconditionally loved there. One of the saddest days of my life was six years ago, when I was ten: Grammy died of a stroke, my anguish compounded by the fact that I wasn't there to hold her hand while her soul left this world and passed on to heaven.

Grammy had bought the unicorn for me soon after our cultural endeavor. I loved that unicorn, but it contained something inside which I loved even more. Whenever I felt trapped in my lonely life, I would hold the figurine up to the light and watch the rainbow escape from its carefully constructed prism prison. Rainbows always seem to yearn for freedom, liberated for only a few minutes after the rage of a thunderstorm or from a crystal cell when a beam of light hits just right. I liked to free the rainbow daily from the unicorn, which guarded it jealously inside its body, and let it bask in the sunlight on the windowsill like an aging cat. I had been just about to do that when Dad came in and slapped it from my hands, sending it soaring. Maybe he thought it was Pegasus the flying horse instead of a unicorn. Whatever the case, after Dad left, I placed the now-mere-horse on the sill and was pleased that it could still grudgingly permit the rainbow its few moments of liberty.

One of my last memories of Grammy, before Mom and Dad came back to snatch me away from my sanctuary, was when she gave me another one of my most precious possessions. She had pulled me into her bedroom one morning, shut the door, and locked it quietly behind us, so as not to wake up my older brother, Irvine, who was still asleep down the hall.

"Shhhh," Grammy said, as she pulled a cardboard shoebox with a picture of old lady shoes on the side from the shelf in her closet. "I have something for you, but you must promise to keep it a secret. Especially from your parents and your brother."

"But why, Grammy?"

"They'd just use it for getting into trouble." She nodded and winked slowly and meaningfully. It took a little while to sink in, but I finally realized she was talking about drugs.

"Okay, I promise."

She opened the box to reveal a pair of old lady shoes, identical to the ones in the picture on the box. I was slightly disappointed and more than a little confused. How could anyone use old lady shoes to buy anything, least of all drugs? But Grammy had a few surprises up her orthopedic shoes, and I would soon realize that sometimes the most drab and mundane things can hold the most amazing treasures. From one shoe, she pulled out a small handgun but quickly put it back, saying, "Oops, wrong shoe" and then, eyeing my startled expression, said with a wink, "You never know when you'll need protection." Then she reached into the other shoe and pulled out a wad of white tissue paper, the kind you stuff in gift bags to hide the present or cram in your shoes so they hold their shape when you're not wearing them.

Grammy put the gloriously ordinary shoes back in the box and the box back on the shelf, then took the wad of paper to her bed. There, as she peeled back the layers of tissue, she revealed the most astonishing thing—a large, round, perfectly clear diamond. It immediately spewed a tricolor rainbow onto Grammy's white chenille bedspread. Grammy said it was nearly a full carat and worth over two thousand dollars. "Save it for when you're old enough to escape."

"But Grammy, I can always just come here," I said with ten-year-old innocence.

"You may not always be able to come here, child of my heart." Grammy liked to call me that because I was not her biological granddaughter. Dad—her son—was really my stepdad, although he was the only father I had ever known and by all accounts was better than my deadbeat biological father who, among many other faults, was physically and emotionally abusive to my mother. Apparently, he suffered from mental illness too. How I was able to avoid the double genetic whammy, I'll never know, but I do wonder if someday I might start hearing demons in my mind as well.

It was Dad—my step-dad—who rescued Mom, toddler Irvine, and fetal me from a lifetime of coldhearted brutality. For all Dad's problems, he had never been physically abusive, and I know deep down, under the layers of insanity and substance-abuse-rot, he really loved Mom, and by accepting responsibility for Irvine and me, tenuous as it was at times, he loved us too.

And that's why I would always forgive him.

Chapter 2

Spiders, Lilacs, and Hogs

PF Day. What can I say about Power Failure Day? Except that it happened three years ago on November 1st when I was thirteen. And it changed my life forever. As if my life wasn't messed up enough already, the sun decided to spew a huge mass of electromagnetic particles at the earth, resulting in the demise of the world's entire power grid. Everything run by electricity or electronics—computers (which ran everything, you know), most automobiles, all manufacturing—zapped in a split second as the electromagnetic pulse of a coronal mass ejection from the sun spread and conquered the geomagnetic shield, which normally protects the earth like a mother's arms around her small child. But like a giant gravid spider, the pulse infiltrated and spread its spindly legs around the earth, releasing its tiny spiderlings, each an exact replica of their mama, to claim the power lines for their webs.

Spiders and webs were what I was doodling in class with my right hand while I took Biology notes with my left just before the power went off. Anyone who had been paying attention in science class knows that spiders are arachnids, gravid means pregnant, and the sun is made of ever-burning, ever-churning, ever-spewing hot plasma. I like spiders. Hot plasma, not so much. But who knows? In the end, it may end up being the catalyst I've needed to make my escape.

Shortly after PF Day, my parents were released from jail with the admonishment to stay in the area because as soon as the power was back on, they'd have to return to finish their sentences. Yeah, right. I expected Mom and Dad to flee as far from Missouri as they could get on foot. But I was wrong. Irv and I were surprised and even a little shocked to find Mom and Dad on the doorstep of the relatives we had been staying with since their incarceration. Dad's cousin Lori and her husband Bob invited Mom and Dad to stay, as we had long since lost the lease on our house. The landlord had sold most of our possessions to pay for back rent.

But Dad had another idea—Uncle Owen's hog farm six and a half miles outside of town. He warned us not to tell anyone about it though. I had visited Uncle Owen's hog farm before and hated it. In fact, there was nowhere on earth I'd less like to be than Uncle Owen's hog farm.

The stench can be detected from a mile away and at the farm it's overpowering. I wanted to try to dissuade him from his odoriferous scheme, but he was adamant, and I wasn't willing to rouse the demons by arguing with him. The hog farm was to be our new home. He was sure Uncle Owen would welcome us. Uncle Owen, being childless and recently a widower, had been trying to get his nephew to go into the hog business with him since Dad was a teen.

A week after PF Day, we arrived at the Hog farm on foot, pulling our meager belongings behind us in a garden cart and a child's red wagon. The odor almost made me turn back and make a break for it long before the farm came into sight, but I held my nose and breathed through my mouth until I felt lightheaded. The fetid smell seemed not to affect my parents and Irv. Their senses of smell were probably eaten away by all the powdered poison they had snuffed before PF Day.

As Dad suspected, Uncle Owen was ecstatic to see us as he was in poor health and badly needed the help. He was a kind old gentleman and allowed me to pick out my room first. I chose an upstairs room on the south side of the house, away from the hog pens, a room under which grew a huge old lilac bush. At least I would have two or three weeks of heady fragrance in the spring to help mask the odor of hogs. Spring was six months away though, I thought sadly.

Since it was November, the putrid smell wasn't as unbearable as in the heat of the summer, but it still made me queasy. After I unpacked my suitcase of clothes—mostly hand-me-downs from cousin Lori's grown daughter—and my cardboard box of the few precious possessions I could carry, I sprayed one of Grammy's handkerchiefs—she always called it her hankie—with a tiny spritz of her cologne, then held it up to my nose and inhaled the scent of *White Diamonds* while memories of Grammy stung my eyes and my heart. They were the only things I took from her house after her funeral. Well, those and the old lady shoes, complete with box and handgun and a small box of bullets. Don't ask me the caliber—I know science and math and English, history and geography and Latin, but I know nothing about guns. Still, as Grammy said, you never know when you might need protection.

I don't like hogs. I like bacon and ham and pork chops, but I don't like the animal they come from. Hogs stink. And they're mean. Uncle Owen spent the first evening we were there showing us his hog scars by candlelight. His left calf looked like a piece of weathered driftwood where an angry sow had chomped a large portion of it off years before, and his right hand was missing half of his pinkie and ring finger from a ravenous boar. Most of the time though, Uncle Owen told us, his hogs were pretty nice. In fact, some of them were like pets to him; he had names for each of his favorites, the breeders who weren't going to slaughter anytime soon. They were nice enough as long as they were fed and watered on a regular basis, which was getting harder and harder for him to do, both because of his age and health, but also because PF Day meant he couldn't use his tractor to haul the feed, and water didn't pour forth from the taps anymore—it had to be pumped from the old well and carried in buckets. But I didn't trust the hogs anyway. And I sure as hell wasn't going to make them pets. I called them names like Chitlin, Sausage, and Pork Chop, just to let them know what I really thought of them.

As I lay on my bed, inhaling memories of Grammy, I watched spiders crawl across my ceiling. Grammy was never afraid of spiders and neither am I. She always said that they were good for eating all the annoying bugs like flies and mosquitoes. I named my spiders Boris and Wolfie and I-Spy. I watched as they spun their webs and waited for some unsuspecting insect to fly into them, the wait stretching out longer and longer as autumn turned to winter. They were quiet, unassuming companions that I could talk to and marvel at. The best thing of all was that Mom, Dad, and even Irv were afraid of them and would usually leave my room when they saw one. When that happened, I'd wink at the spider and whisper, "Good job, Boris."

The first few days at Uncle Owen's were not bad for Mom and Dad. They had been able to score some "ice" immediately after they'd left the jail, so they were okay. They had to ration it somewhat, but Uncle Owen had plenty of booze to make up for it. Poor Irv, though. My parents wouldn't share their stash and repeatedly denied even having any, so Irv was faced with the agony of withdrawal soon after PF Day. Whenever I felt sorry for myself, I thought about what my poor brother was going through and transferred my pity to him. At barely fifteen, he began to look like an old man, withered and hollow inside. I suppose that's what he was. Isn't that why people start using in the first place? Dad had his voices, Mom had her life-crushing sadness, but what did Irv have at such a young age that made him want to be someone or something else through the escape of a temporary high?

When Irv and I were younger, before the ice

took ahold of his heart too, I used to ask him why Mom and Dad seemed to care about their drugs more than us. He told me I thought too much. He said it didn't matter, it was what it was, and that was that. Not much of an answer, I thought. But that was the major difference between Irv and me then, besides the sixteen months difference in our ages—I thought too much, he not enough. Maybe if he had thought more, he'd have realized how destructive drugs and alcohol are and decided to stay away from them like I did. Now the major difference between us is that the only ice I like is in a glass of Dr. Pepper.

And oh, how I yearn for a nice cold glass of that sweet ambrosia! I haven't had one since the day before PF Day. That spewing, churning, conquering, life-altering day.

Chapter 3

Types of Survival

What exactly constitutes survival? I feel like I've been barely surviving my whole life. At a very young age, I was left alone to forage for food while my brother got himself up and off to kindergarten and my parents lay catatonic on the bed, couch, or floor—wherever they had passed out. I learned how to make a breakfast of stale chips and moldy bread while I watched cartoons over their near-lifeless bodies. That is until the TV got repossessed. After that, I taught myself to read the books that Irv brought home from school. I'd often hide them between the couch cushions so he wouldn't take them back to school before I had memorized them.

I figured out how to melt into the background when Mom and Dad were awake, so they wouldn't take out the pain of their hangovers on me. I also learned how to hang onto very few possessions and to keep them with a change of clothing in a backpack, so I'd be ready to move at a moment's notice, either when my parents were running from the police or when the cops caught up to them and hauled them to jail. It was easier to grab that small bag when the lady from Child Protective Services came to get Irv and me than to frantically try to pack a bunch of things and risk forgetting something special. Usually, when we finally were able to return home, it was to a different house, empty of any of the possessions we had amassed at the previous one.

But not long after PF Day, survival became so much harder. We had it easy at Uncle Owen's farm compared to a lot of people. We had food to eat, water to pump, and wood to burn in the old Buck stove, which heated the downstairs where everyone else slept. I didn't mind being cold upstairs though. The colder it was, the less the hogs reeked and the less often my parents visited my room, so being cold was fine with me.

Many people in town didn't have any way to heat their homes or to cook their food, if they even had any to cook. Water was hard to come by too. I felt bad for the people in town, but I also envied them because they had normal families to take care of each other. I have always envied everyone else. That's why I never had any real friends. Sure, it was hard to make friends when everyone else's parents knew about my parents' drug use and wouldn't let their kids come over to my house. But it was more than that. When I was younger, I was so jealous of their normal childhoods that I hated them. As I got older I realized that it wasn't their fault and I forgave them for their familial serendipity. I like that word—*serendipity*. It's a word that belongs in their world though, not mine. It used to belong to the world of the glass unicorn too, before his flight that made him a mere-horse. Words like *serendipity*, *normal*, and *family* describe why I couldn't get close to anyone; Irv and Grammy were my only true friends.

Uncle Owen gave me a wall calendar and I carefully marked off each day, not because I cared at all what day it was, but just because it was something to do. Even though I helped with the everyday chores of hauling water to the house, cooking meals, and keeping things tidy—I flat-out refused to do anything with the hogs—I spent a large part of every day in my room alone. Luckily, Uncle Owen's late wife, Aunt Helen, loved to read, and he had kept all her books, so besides the spiders, I had plenty of book-friends to keep me company. I wasn't really lonely; I was used to being alone. At this point, life and survival wasn't too bad. But that was about to change.

In mid November, roughly two weeks after

PF Day, the ice and booze ran out. We were about to embark on an experience worthy of *The Hunger Games*, a fight to the death for the inhabitants of our malodorous arena. I wasn't too keen on entering the fray—well, who is anyway? Like Katniss, my strategy was to lie low and wait the others out, which worked to some extent. The only problem though was that unlike Katniss's situation, I was related to all the other contestants in the game and I didn't want to see any of them hurt.

The first casualty was Uncle Owen, although it was due more to his previous bad health and the absence of his heart medication than the combative atmosphere of his once peaceful home. That morning he was trying to talk Dad into helping him kill and butcher a hog. In his calm, patient manner, he was explaining that it would provide meat as well as tallow for candles to last through the winter in case the electricity didn't come back on soon, which it was beginning to look like it wasn't. I listened at the top of the stairs, hidden from the conversation below, testing the temperature of their moods before plunging in. Dad, in the throes of his withdrawal and under the influence of the phantom voices in his head, was hard to convince. It was only after Uncle Owen promised to do most of the work, having Dad there just for safety, that Dad agreed. The conversation sounded like Dad was being lazy or squeamish about the killing, but I suspected the real reason was that he was afraid that the blood and gore of slaughter would excite the demons that were beginning to take control of him.

Mom and I were cleaning up the kitchen after the men went out to perform their gruesome task. After half an hour or so, we both jumped when we heard a single gunshot, then laughed nervously, thinking that it was just the demise of the hog. Several minutes later however, Dad and Irv came in alone, both white-faced and visibly shaken. Irv made a beeline for his room without saying anything, but Dad sat in Uncle Owen's chair with his head in his hands. After a few tense seconds, he said in a leaden voice, "Owen's dead." Then he jumped up and went to his room, with Mom trailing behind like a lost child.

I stood frozen for a few minutes, trying to make sense of what he'd said but failing that, I decided to ask Irv and went to his room, where he lay on his bed, looking up at the ceiling.

"So… Uncle Owen's really dead?" I asked.

"Yeah."

"What happened?" I asked timidly, half afraid the answer would be that Dad had killed him.

"I don't know. His heart, I guess."

I sat on the bed next to Irv. He sighed and sat up beside me, knowing I wasn't going to leave until he told me the whole story.

"He was in the hog pen trying to separate the one we were going to slaughter from the rest of them," he explained. "Suddenly he clutched at his chest, looked at us like he was pleading for our help, and then he fell to the ground. Dad and I tried to get to him, but the hogs surrounded him for some reason and acted like they wanted to kill us. So we got out of the pen and Dad picked up the shotgun and shot it over their heads to scare them off."

"Did it work?"

"Yeah." He didn't say anything else as he stared at his shaking hands in his lap.

"So… Was he already dead when you went in there?"

"Yeah."

His verbal reluctance was getting tedious. I tried to be patient as I mentally opened his mouth, reached down his throat, and pulled out the words. "So what did you do?"

"I tried to pull him out of there, but I couldn't budge him."

"You just left him there?" I asked, incredulously. "How do you know he was dead?"

"I could tell… He died with his eyes open."

“Oh, you mean ‘windows of the soul’ and all.”

“Yeah, except there was no soul in those eyes. There was nothing at all in those eyes.”

I thought about that for a few seconds, the image of lifeless eyes beginning to spook me. “Were you scared?”

Irv was trying to summon some bravado, but in the end he told me the truth, like always. His shoulders sagged as he admitted, “Hell yes, I was scared. I don’t know if I was more scared of the hogs or those dead eyes.”

I shuddered and put my arm around my big brother. I wanted to shield him from the pain and the memories, but I really didn’t know how.

Chapter 4

Ghosts

The next morning, Irv had to go out and feed the hogs because Dad wouldn't get up. I know my brother was terrified of encountering Uncle Owen's lifeless body again, but he was also scared of facing Dad's anger if he didn't do it. So out he went. I stood by the back door, waiting for him, worried about him but not enough to go out there with him.

After a half an hour or so, he came back in, his face white as a ghost. I again followed him to his bedroom where he divulged his experience in the hog pen.

"Uncle Owen's body is gone," he said unevenly.

"What?" My voice was as high as my eyebrows.

"There were a few pieces of his clothing lying around, but no body." He looked at me with round spooked eyes.

"The hogs?" I was disgusted and anguished at the same time.

"I don't know. The hogs were locked in another pen. I don't know how they would have got in there. Maybe Dad…"

"You think he did it? Buried him, I mean?"

"Maybe…"

As creeped out as I was, thinking about how Uncle Owen's body had disappeared, I couldn't help wondering about it all day long. When Dad finally got up late in the afternoon, he merely said he had taken care of the body. His exact words were, "I took care of it. Can't have his body around inviting his ghost to stay here."

He must have done it during one of his midnight haunts, as none of us heard or saw him do it during the day. That left me to speculate about the various ways Dad could have taken care of it. #1 Dad could have chased the hogs into the other pen then buried the body, but that would have been so much work for one man and there was no evidence of disturbed earth where he would have been buried. #2 Dad burned the body, but we couldn't see any place where the ground was charred. #3 The hogs ate the body, and then Dad chased them into the other pen. The latter option seemed the most likely in my mind, even though it made me squeamish to think about it. I made a pact with myself to never eat the meat from those hogs, just in case. I wouldn't want to have a piece of

Uncle Owen's spirit floating around in me.

Which made me start to think about ghosts. The idea of ghosts has always intrigued me. Do we all have a ghost of ourselves that lives inside us until we die? The preachers at the churches we'd go to when Mom and Dad would miraculously find God after a stint in rehab, before they would find God in their drugs again, called it our spirit. They made it sound like our spirit was a good thing, loving and beautiful. But everywhere else, you hear that spirits or ghosts are bad and hang around to haunt you and make your life miserable. It made me wonder if Dad's mind was full of ghosts or spirits other than his own. Did Grammy's ghost inhabit his head? Would Uncle Owen's be rattling around in there now too? Or were Dad's ghosts all bad ghosts, little devils telling him to do bad things? I wasn't afraid of Dad, but I was a little spooked by the ghosts haunting him. Poor Dad. He really must be a good man to have kept all those ghosts at bay for so long.

A few days later, Dad decided that a hog needed to be slaughtered. We had plenty of jars of fruits and vegetables that Aunt Helen had canned before she died, but Dad wanted meat, and the meat from Uncle Owen's big freezer had run out or gone bad. So Dad made Irv single out a fat hog and shoot it. Then Dad took over, hacking it to pieces while Irv carted it off to the smokehouse a few pieces at a time. Apparently, Dad had gotten over his fear of violence because he tore into that carcass like it was everyone who'd ever done him wrong. I watched from the kitchen window, at once horrified and fascinated; I couldn't tear my eyes away until the last bloody piece was loaded into the wheelbarrow. Irv looked pale and old. His hands shook while he picked up the chunks of meat and waited for the next piece to load. I should have gone out to help him, but I couldn't force myself to move. I still watched as he frantically pumped frigid water to wash his hands when his gruesome task was complete. Or maybe it wasn't he who was frantic, but my own mind, which wanted him to be rid of the evidence before the ghost of Uncle Owen could find him and inhabit his fragile mind.

Dad came in with a big chunk of pork, hollering for Mom to cook it for him. Mom was taking one of her frequent naps and couldn't be awoken even though Dad shook her, so the task of cooking defaulted to me. When I showed reluctance to cut the chunk into manageable pork chops, Dad impatiently sliced it up, his hands flying so fast I was sure he'd cut off one of his fingers. I didn't find any spare digits in the meat as I cooked it, so I guess he was okay. As the meat cooked in the big cast iron skillet atop the Buck stove, I had a vision of Uncle Owen's ephemeral form floating up from the chops like a genie from a bottle, my nose inhaling him as I breathed in the enticing aroma. I held my breath and tied a towel around the lower part of my face. Just in case.

After a quick lunch of home-canned green beans and peaches, I decided to take a cleansing walk. I thought if I walked far enough away from the farm, the chilly air might expunge the odor of hogs and death from my nostrils and my psyche. I loaded a backpack with some items I thought I might need: a pocketknife, some wooden matches, a bottle of fresh well water, a field guide to native flora and fauna from Aunt Helen's library, etc. At the last minute, I threw in a small store-bought can of deviled ham—ironic, I know, since I had sworn off pork, but I figured the intense processing of this pork product would dispel any ghosts hanging around and the sealed can would keep them out. Try as I might to avoid temptation, the memory of the aroma of those pork chops cooking was like an invisible finger poking at my brain, beckoning me to try a little. I tried not to believe it could be Uncle Owen knocking at my subconscious.

Chapter 5

Foraging

The first time I walked into the woods, an inexplicable feeling of peace blanketed my mind. I purposely chose the woods to the west of the farm so that the prevailing winds would blow the stench of the hogs away, but I was filled with trepidation as I crept along the length of the hog pen nearest the house to get to the tree line. The hogs in that pen eyed me suspiciously—or was it voraciously?—especially one beady-eyed black one who walked sideways along the fence in order to always be facing me, glaring at me the entire way. It gave me a queasy feeling. Was this the one that had eaten Uncle Owen? Was Uncle Owen's ghost angry with me or just trying to communicate?

At any rate, my frenzied mind suddenly relaxed in the shadows of the trees as if they stood as guardians against the ghosts that trailed me and I could be relieved of that duty. I inhaled the fresh earthy aromas as my frantic pace slowed to a stroll. I felt at home for the first time since Grammy died.

After almost an hour of wandering, I found a huge fallen tree and sat on its rotting trunk to rest and take in my surroundings. I had not thought of the possibility of getting lost—or maybe I had, subconsciously, and followed my hidden desire. But now, sitting on the log and taking stock of my odds of survival all alone in an unfamiliar woods at the start of winter, I realized that the odds were not in my favor. Besides, I needed to stay around the farm to watch over my family, even though I really didn't know at all how to help them.

I opened my backpack and took out the deviled ham, peeled back the pull-tab, and used my tongue to pry out the juicy, salty contents, gulping it down like a ravenous, cannibalistic pig. I chuckled to myself, thinking about how I had outwitted the hog-ghosts by eating canned pork.

After I ate, I pulled out the field guide and began to leaf through it, pausing when I recognized the bark of a tree I had passed or a particular kind of nut I had stepped over on my way through the woods. The clues were few at this time of year since the leaves and fruits were mostly gone, but I was able to identify trees with distinctive bark like sycamore (pale and white like it's sick), shagbark hickory (shaggy), and paper birch (papery). I also easily identified pine trees because of their needles. I read in the guide that pine needles can be used to make a tea that is an excellent source of vitamin C. I decided to collect some pine needles, acorns, and walnuts to take home to supplement my canned food diet.

One page of the field guide especially caught my attention. It described how the inner bark of the white willow contains salicin, which can be used in place of aspirin for various aches and pains. Maybe that would help Irvine, I thought, and I made it my mission to find a willow tree to harvest the pain reliever for my tortured brother. In the margin, Aunt Helen had written in barely legible scribbles—*good for arthritis*—as if she had actually tried it.

As I searched for willows, I thought about sweet Aunt Helen and how she was still giving me what I needed. I remembered her as a kind, down-to-earth old lady with an ample bosom that seemed to engulf me as she hugged me. Even though I enjoyed the hug and craved that simple act of connection, I felt I could suffocate if the hug went on too long. I'm sure Irv enjoyed it much more than I. He always wore a goofy grin when he resurfaced from one of her hugs.

I realized in the woods that day that Aunt Helen had been the only bright spot to otherwise miserable visits to the hog farm. She had fed us, stroked our meager funny bones, and showed us some of the old ways, like "putting up" fruits and vegetables and dehydrating meat. More importantly, she had made Irv and me feel like we belonged to an extended family, and that is something I cherish to this day even though that feeling died with her and Grammy.

It took a some time and hiking to finally locate a stand of willows by a little creek trickling through the woods. I chose the biggest, healthiest-looking one and carefully peeled back a piece of the bark. The inner bark was pinkish white. I stripped off a good amount and stowed it in the backpack. I also found pine needles and nuts to add to my harvest.

It was late afternoon and the sun was beginning to sink behind the tress. I decided I should probably head back home, so I reluctantly put the setting sun behind me and headed east. As I walked, I wondered if anyone would have missed me since I was gone longer than I had realized and I hadn't told anyone that I was leaving. I was concerned that Mom would be worried about me. Wishful thinking, perhaps, as I didn't really believe she would come out of her fog enough to even know I was missing. At least Irvine would be concerned, I was sure.

It was nearly dark when I made it back

home. Irvine was waiting for me on the stoop and rose to meet me halfway across the yard as I hurried past the hog pen. He didn't say anything, merely stopping in front of me and looking me over. When he was satisfied that I was unharmed, he turned and headed back to the house. He didn't need to say anything or even to hug me for me to know that he cared about me. He was the only one who had even noticed that I was gone.

Later that evening, I made him a steaming cup of tea from the inner bark of the willow. He didn't ask why or say that it helped him in any way, but I felt that I had paid him back for his concern for me. I hoped it at least helped him sleep without pain for a while.

Chapter 6

Town

Early in December, Irv decided he wanted to walk to town and asked me to go with him. The odd look in his eyes and the tremor in his voice led me to believe he was desperately hoping to score some drugs in town. Part of me hoped he would, if only to ease his withdrawal pain and make him somewhat happy again. But mostly I hoped the 'ice' had all melted with the sun's fury on PF Day.

We walked at a brisk pace matched by the bracing wind blowing against our backs, past abandoned vehicles and eerily quiet farms. While I felt invigorated by the clean crisp sweetness of the chilly air, I could hear Irv's teeth chattering and looked over to see him shivering despite Uncle Owen's fur-lined hat and voluminous coat, which wrapped around Irv one-and-a-half times.

To keep his mind off his suffering, I started a conversation, rather one-sided as usual. "Do you ever think of getting away? From them, I mean." I wasn't sure whether by 'them' I meant

Mom and Dad, the hogs, or the ghosts—probably a culmination of all of them. I decided to let Irv draw his own conclusions though.

"Yeeaah." He drew out the word like he was reluctant to let it go. It had a little lilt at the end, which I took to mean he wanted to know more of what I was thinking. Either way, I was going to tell him.

"We could move back in with Lori and Bob. Or maybe find a place of our own in town." I wiggled my raised eyebrows to make the ideas more tempting. It didn't work.

"He'd just come to get us back. He needs help on the farm." Wow, the most words he'd said in months and they were to dash my hopes and dreams. But I knew he was right.

When we got to town, I followed Irv around like a puppy as he visited his dealers, trying to score some relief. All said the same thing—the ice had run out shortly after PF Day and there was no way to get any more. The best bet, they told him, was to make some alcohol by fermenting grain or fruit. It would take several days, but it was something to look forward to at least. The last guy we visited gave Irv step-by-step instructions for which Irv gave him a wad of cash. Those dealers knew how to get money from the junkies even without selling them drugs. I would have given the knowledge away for free if I had known about it.

We visited Bob and Lori just to say hello. Lori kept wringing her hands, saying she felt bad that she couldn't offer us anything to eat. I told her to come visit us on the farm to get some pork and canned goods, which made her start to cry. I imagined it was because the tables had turned so drastically—once they were the ones we could count on for stability and the normal necessities of life, but now they would have to rely on us.

Bob, who worked for the electric company, told us about his trip to Kansas City to find parts to fix the blown transformers right after PF Day and the chaos that had already begun to engulf that metropolis. He told about riots and assaults and murders, as if the thirst, starvation, and diseases were not enough to demoralize the already traumatized population. But there was more. Rampant, out-of-control fires, lack of sanitation, and the release of prisoners and the mentally ill put even more stress on the inhabitants of the city. Bob estimated that half the city's population wouldn't survive the winter if electricity wasn't restored soon. He added solemnly that there were not enough parts to fix the power grid soon though, since the whole country had been affected. It was the first time we heard that the power failure was at least countrywide and that it was going to be quite a while before the power was back on. It made me start thinking about long-term survival.

After that, Irv and I walked around town to see what was going on. The houses were dark and seemed to huddle forlornly against the wind. The few businesses in our small town were closed, some with boarded-up windows to deter looters. I was beginning to think it had become a ghost town. Would I ever get away from ghosts?

Nearing the town square, we heard muffled sounds carried on the wind, like people talking but not quite, reinforcing the idea of ghosts inhabiting the town. We finally found a large group of people—real live people, not ghosts—milling around tables of wares, talking and bartering. I was more relieved then I would have thought as I don't normally like to be around lots of people, but compared to ghosts, I'll take people every time, even though the townspeople, many of whom I'd known most of my life, looked more like skeletons from lack of food or zombies from the trauma of the situation than how I remembered them.

Irv now distractedly followed me, as I wandered around looking at what people were selling or trading, and listening in on conversations to get information about the electricity situation as well as some tips on survival.

At Mrs. Littleton's table—she owns a greenhouse at the edge of town—I stopped and eavesdropped as she discussed medicinal plants with Bracken Powell's mom, Lauren. For a few desperate moments, I daydreamed that Lauren was my real mother and that she would recognize me and want me to come live with her. She was so kind and loving and their family was so normal—the kind of normal I'd been craving all my life.

Lauren interrupted my beautiful reverie by asking if I was interested in herbs too, and it took me a second to realize that my dream hadn't really come true, that she was just being her friendly self by including me in the conversation.

I told her that I'd like to learn more and she and Mrs. Littleton were more than happy to educate me. Mrs. Littleton even gave me a book about Missouri plants that can be used for medicinal purposes.

After a long conversation with the ladies—perhaps the longest I'd ever talked to anyone—I looked around for Irv so we could reluctantly start heading home. He wasn't in the square, so I wandered around town until I found him a few blocks away talking to a bunch of kids from school. At my signal, he silently disengaged from the group and joined me, and like ghosts, we slipped away without anyone noticing.

When we arrived home, it was as if we'd never left, or more precisely, that we were never there in the first place, because mom acted as though she didn't even see us at all. I had a fleeting thought that maybe we really had become ghosts.

Chapter 7

Mom

How I longed for a mother who worried over me, gave me chores and discipline, made my life pseudo-miserable like normal mothers did. Before PF Day, whenever I had heard kids complain about their mothers not letting them do something, or making them do their homework instead of hanging out with friends, or embarrassing them by showing up at school with their forgotten lunch money, or a million other things that normal mothers apparently do, I wanted to scream, "You're so lucky your mom cares about you!"

Instead, my mother didn't care what I did or didn't do, whom I hung out with, whether I even had anything to eat. She relied on the 'system' to raise me. She did as little as she could possibly get by with to keep Irvine and me alive. There were no hugs, no bedtime stories, no tenderness for us. It was as if she wished we had never been born.

Still, I had glimpses from time to time that Mom did love us. Like the time she had to meet with my teacher at the end of my third grade year after it had been determined that I had a learning disability in math.

"As you know, Mrs. Smith, I think Taylor has enormous potential. We just haven't been able to tap into it yet," Mrs. Allen told Mom. I sat beside Mom, imagining my 'potential' spilling out of me like a giant rainbow, filling up all the dark corners of the room like multi-colored enlightenment.

"However," she continued, "most children can multiply and divide by the end of third grade, yet Taylor is still struggling. The test results confirm what I've been suspecting all along: Taylor has dyscalculia."

"So are you going to help her now?" Mom asked. "Give her a tutor or special classes or something?"

"Well now, therein lies the conundrum." I'm sure Mom didn't know what that meant, but she covered her vocabulary shortcomings with a steady gaze. Mrs. Allen continued. "Taylor's IQ is very high, too high to qualify for federally-funded programming, and I'm afraid our small school district just doesn't have the resources to help either."

Mom's face changed almost imperceptibly from serene listener to cold inquisitor. When she spoke, her voice matched her expression, and Mrs. Allen was taken aback. "What does IQ have to do with learning disabilities? Taylor needs help; she deserves to get help."

"Oh, yes, Mrs. Smith. I totally agree."

"Then help her," Mom insisted.

"I'm afraid you will have to give her the extra attention she needs, Mrs. Smith. We just don't have the resources to help her."

"What do you do with the kids who have learning disabilities and low IQs?"

"We get money from the government for special tutors for them," the teacher answered between lips frozen into a determined smile.

"Then it's easy. Just let Taylor sit with the other students during their tutoring sessions. Problem solved." And with that, Mom stood up and left the room, not even checking to see if I followed. I stole a glance at Mrs. Allen before scampering after Mom; she looked perplexed, as if not sure whether to argue the point or accept it. Then she sighed and I knew she had given up.

I started visiting the tutor during math class the next day. Although Mom never asked how I was doing in math, I did improve until I finally figured it out in the fourth grade. From then on, I never had trouble with any subject in school.

Another time the mother bear hidden inside Mom's indifference came out was once when

Child Protective Services came to visit to check up on our welfare. The social worker was a persnickety older lady who was apparently not happy with the state of my wardrobe. She made a disparaging remark about me looking like an orphan, to which Mom icily replied, "She is not an orphan; she's my beautiful angel no matter how she's dressed!"

I hold on to those memories like Grammy's diamond.

As I looked at Mom now, I wondered how she had gotten old so fast. The lines on her face seemed deeper and the new hair growth since PF day was totally gray. When had she started coloring her hair to cover the gray? I knew she colored her hair, but I thought it was because she liked to change her appearance, maybe to throw off the police. I didn't know she *needed* to color it. After all, she was only 34.

Now she and, in fact, many of the women in town looked like some giant Van Gogh had dipped the tops of their heads in varying shades of gray paint to use as paintbrushes for some huge impressionist work of art, which to me was almost beautiful in itself. I have always been drawn to Van Gogh's work, not only because of his bold and quirky style, but also because of the fascinating back-story of mental illness that fueled his visions.

I'd always thought Mom was pretty, but I wasn't so sure now. In fact, my whole idea of 'pretty' had changed drastically since PF Day. The girls in town that had been considered 'pretty' before PF Day, with their makeup, salon-styled hair, and latest fashions, now looked drab and downright homely next to girls like Skylar Tipton, a natural beauty who used to be dismissed as ho-hum because she didn't adorn herself with all the trappings of fake beauty like the popular girls. I was glad I had always stayed true to what nature and God had given me, so I didn't miss the beauty products. The fake beauties were now desperate for makeup and hair-styling products—so desperate they were even trading food for it.

I made a note to myself to look for any products of Mom's or Aunt Helen's I could find at home to give the girls next time I was in town. Not to ingratiate myself with them, but because I felt bad for envying them in the past.

Chapter 8

Sanctuary

A few days later, the suffocating atmosphere of Mom's indifference and Dad's paranoia got the better of me, so I headed to the woods to the west of the farm again to clear my head and escape the feeling of impending doom that had settled over our lives. As before, the woods were calming and protective, and I felt renewed hope in surviving our situation beyond the eventual return of the power grid.

When I left for the woods, I could hear Irv tinkering in one of the outbuildings—the one farthest from the house and closest to the woods. I didn't stop to ask him what he was doing because I wanted to be alone and didn't want to risk him deciding to accompany me, as unlikely as that was. Even though I loved my brother and felt closer to him than anyone else on earth, he had demons of his own, and I was just tired of playing the part of Don Quixote, fighting not the imaginary giants, but the all-too-real 'windmills' of mental illness, addiction, and ghosts.

I was on a mission that day as well. In the book of medicinal plants that Mrs. Littleton had given me, I found one—milk thistle—that helps detoxify the liver, which is especially important for alcohol and drug abusers. It also listed dandelion plants as good for that. Since it was early winter, I wasn't sure I'd be able to find any, but it had been unseasonably warm and the grass was still green despite chilly nights and occasional cooler days—such is Missouri's capricious weather—so I held out a little hope anyway.

As I walked slowly along the meager trail made by wild animals, I inhaled the fragrance of the woods, the essence of the earth itself. Evergreens, musty fallen leaves, and the slight musky scent of animals were such a refreshing change from the cloying scents of hogs and mental illness. Not many people realize that mental illness has an odor of its own. It's the smell of desperation and decay, fear and isolation. As much as I loathed the odor of hogs, the smell that permeated the house with desolation was much worse.

In a small clearing, I paused to enjoy the thin light and warmth from the sun peeking between the tops of the trees, and my eyes followed a ray of sunlight to a patch of dandelion plants in the middle of the clearing. They were ragged and limp from the cold but still green, albeit a dark ashy green, so I plucked several plants, roots and all, and stashed them in my backpack. I was careful to leave a few plants so that I could come back in the spring for the new growth, which would be especially good for nutrition and medicine.

While I was digging, I thought I heard the crunching of fallen leaves like someone or something was walking through the woods behind me. I spun around, half expecting Irv to be stalking me and half afraid that the ghosts had infiltrated my safe zone. I couldn't see anything out of place and didn't hear the sound again so I finally went back to digging, thinking that my overactive imagination had just played a trick on me.

Just as I finished my harvest, I heard the sound again, this time making the hair on the back of my neck stand up out of some kind of primal instinct. At first I was frozen in fear, but then a flush of white-hot anger flooded my system with adrenaline. I suppose 'fight' won out over 'flight' as I subconsciously thought about losing my sanctuary to fear. I stood abruptly and swung around to face where the sound came from, shouting, "Come out and face me, spook!"

A shadow, a movement in the leaves beyond the clearing, caught my eye. I stared at the spot, willing my eyes to bore into the gloom to ferret out my antagonist. Nothing. No movement, no sound.

After a few tense moments, which seemed like minutes, I relaxed, the adrenaline draining from my system as fast as it had came, leaving me weak and unsteady. I sat down cross-legged and put my chin in my hands, still vigilant but not as confrontational. I briefly wondered again if I was losing my sanity.

All of a sudden the leaves parted a bit, and a pair of spooky yellow eyes stared back at me.

Chapter 9
Spook

I shivered slightly, even though I tried as hard as I could to appear strong and stalwart. Suddenly I didn't care anymore, and I allowed my shoulders to slump, signaling my surrender to the spook whose gaze never wavered nor blinked. I thought how weak I was, giving in so easily, nearly inviting the ghost to take over my soul.

But it wasn't a ghost after all. After a few seconds, a gray snout appeared, and then a head, a body, all clad in a silky gray coat that shimmered in the sunlight as it crept into the clearing. Soon I knew what it was that had been watching me, stalking me maybe. A dog. Just a dog, a beautiful, lithe, large gray dog. A Weimeraner to be exact. I'd seen them before on TV while watching the Westminster Kennel Club Dog Show.

After gulping down the disappointment of my weakness, I said in a soft and still quivering voice, "Hi, Spook."

At the sound of my voice, the dog seemed

to come alive and it shook with excitement over meeting a friendly soul. He came right up to me and nudged my face with his nose. I completed the greeting by reaching up to stroke his fur and I couldn't help but chuckle over the tumult of emotions my brain had traversed in just a few seconds.

As I petted his back, I noticed Spook was quite thin, not starving, but his ribs were beginning to feel like an old metal washboard. I reached into my pack and pulled out a tin of Vienna sausages. As I fed them to him one-by-one, forever cementing his devotion to me, I slurped the contents of a jar of home-canned applesauce and laughed as he cleaned up the happy mess on my face.

After our snack, we wandered through the woods together, Spook stuck to my side like I was his long-lost friend. Together we searched for more dandelions and other wild edibles and medicines, finding a few here and there. We were even able to find some milk thistle plants that had gone to seed. I carefully collected the seeds to combine with the dandelion roots for a liver detox tea. I was pleased with myself for finding something to help my family as well as finding a friend to ease my loneliness. Hope filled my body like the rays of sunshine that warmed the chill of the December afternoon.

Before long, my canine companion began walking ahead of me instead of beside me. I followed, believing that Spook was leading me somewhere. We walked for quite a while and I noticed through the trees that the sun was just beginning to slide down the sky toward the west, signaling that it was after noon. I was starting to think about heading back home when we came upon a small cabin in a large clearing in the woods. There was smoke coming out of a small chimney flue on the roof, so I knew someone was living there. Spook seemed to know that too as he went right up onto the porch and scratched at the door while I stood back and watched from the edge of the clearing.

The door opened, but I couldn't see who was on the other side because it only opened wide enough for the dog to enter. A thin voice said something, but it was too hushed for me to make out what was said or what manner of person was talking. Spook started in but hesitated then looked back at me as if to say, "Aren't you coming?"

After an expectant pause, which hung in air like an unfulfilled promise, Spook sat and whined, looking from me to the person in the cabin and back again to me. The door creaked open slowly—or at least it was slow in my imagination—and soon I could see an old woman in the doorway. She hunched her shoulders and stared hard in my direction until I apparently came into focus. When she finally saw me, she straightened up and said, "Well hello, young lady. What brings you this far into the woods?"

I swear, visions of Hansel and Gretel and the old witch flashed through my mind, and I almost turned and ran. But I got ahold of my rampant imagination and worked up the courage to speak. After all, she looked harmless enough and this was the 21st century, not medieval times, even though we had been forced to live like it since PF Day.

"I was just out for a walk and met your dog. He brought me here."

She chuckled, throaty and phlegmy, then coughed a little before answering, "He's not my dog. He just visits sometimes. Don't know who he belongs to."

"Oh. Do you know his name? I've been calling him Spook."

"Spook's as good a name as any. He looks kind of spooky." She cackled again. "Well, don't just stand there, dear, come in and have a cup o' tea with me. I haven't had a human visitor for several months."

As I entered the cabin, my eyes having to adjust to the dim candlelight within, the woman continued to talk, the words pouring out of her mouth like they had been held back too long.

"The last visitor I had was sometime last spring. The granddaughter of my dear friend Vona May came to see how I was doing and to bring me some supplies. You see I've been on my own since my dear husband died two years ago. He was such a dear…" She paused and her eyes misted over as she thought of her 'dears.' Then she snapped out of it and said cheerfully, "My name's Fern. What's yours, dear?"

I was warmed by the fact that she already included me in her 'dears,' so I was eager to converse with this sweet lonely lady. "I'm Taylor Smith."

"Ah, a tinker, a tailor, a candlestick maker…" She laughed heartily at her own joke until she started coughing again. After she caught her breath, she said, "Darn cough. From the wood stove, you know. Anyway, where are you from, dear, and are you lost here so deep in the woods?"

"I'm not lost; I know exactly how to get home from here. Due east."

"Ah, you from town then?"

"Well, sorta. We're staying at Owen Smith's hog farm."

"I remember Owen. Helen is his wife, right? How are they? Good people, Owen and Helen."

"Uh, they both passed away recently. My dad was their nephew."

"Oh, so sorry to hear that, dear. Good people, they were," she repeated. "Well, like I said, my name's Fern and I lived in town years ago. I went to school with Owen and Helen. Well, Helen was a couple of years behind us, but I knew her well enough. Sweet girl. Like you." She smiled warmly at me.

"Thank you." I blushed. "It's nice to meet you, Fern."

"So now tell me why you've strayed so far from the farm, Taylor. It must be two or three miles from here. Seems to me you have a story to tell," she paused slightly, "as do I."

Chapter 10

Fern

At first I was reluctant to share my story with my new friend, but Fern had a way of drawing me out much like I did with Irv. She was surprised when she heard about PF Day as she had lived without electricity for quite some years and had not had a visitor since before the CME changed the way the rest of us lived. I told her about my brother and parents but stopped short of telling her about their past drug abuse and current mental issues. My story was compelling enough even without those tidbits. When she asked again why I was so deep into the woods, I answered honestly that I was trying to escape the ghosts of the people who had died. She nodded in understanding and said, "That's the reason I moved here."

Fern then started telling me her story.

"My Jack, my dear sweet Jack…" her eyes misted over and she wiped them before she continued. "I knew the day I met him that he was my soul mate. We were in college and we never went a day without talking—either in person or on the phone—since the day we met. Until he died, that is." She wiped her eyes again and blew her nose into a white cotton hankie. "Jack was a botanist. He called me his sweet bracken—that means fern, you know." I nodded and the image of Bracken Powell invaded my thoughts, becoming Jack in the movie my mind was making of Fern's story.

"Sometimes I called him my jackass," Fern chuckled, "but usually, I called him 'my dearest' because he was. We never had any children; never knew why. We wanted them, it just never happened. Anyway, after we graduated from college, we bought a house next door to my best friend, Vona May, who had four children already. Oh how I doted on those children. Years later, they grew up and had children of their own. I've stayed close with some of them, especially Vona May's youngest granddaughter, Lauren, who named one of her boys after me…sort of." Fern snorted a laugh as she confirmed my dawning realization, "His name's Bracken. Do you know him?"

"Yes, I do," I said incredulously. "He's in my brother's class."

"Well, sweet Lauren visits me often to make sure I have everything I need out here. She keeps trying to talk me into moving to a senior apartment where her parents live, but I'll stay here as long as I can hold out. So far, so good!" She grinned and waggled her eyebrows, making me laugh out loud.

"In return for Lauren's devotion to me, I teach her about herbal medicines and the old ways of life. I guess that knowledge would come in real handy for people right about now, eh?"

I nodded, more interested than ever in her story, and asked, "How did you lose your husband, if you don't mind me asking?"

"Oh, I don't mind at all, dear," she said as she patted my hand. "I was just getting to that part. Jack and I had a marvelous greenhouse where we raised all sorts of plants, from ornamental, to food, to medicinal. When we retired, we sold it to the Littleton's."

"Yes, I know Mrs. Littleton. And Lauren Powell."

"Oh good, have you seen the greenhouse? It was our pride and joy."

"Yes, it's a beautiful greenhouse. Mrs. Littleton takes good care of it."

"That's so nice to hear, dear. Anyway, Jack built this cabin for hunting and getting away from it all."

"How did you get the building materials here in the woods?"

"Good question. There's an old gravel road

to the west. It used to come clear up to the cabin, but it's so overgrown around here now, you have to walk a few hundred feet to get to it. Now as I was saying, Jack bought this land and this cabin for hunting and fishing—the river's a short hike from here—so we could take mini vacations and practice our love of living in the old way. The more we came here, the more we loved it until we decided to sell our house in town and move out here." She sighed and smiled wistfully. "But before our house sold, he had a heart attack. I tried to save him, did CPR, and the paramedics got there quickly, but we couldn't save him. The coroner told me later the attack was so massive that he probably wouldn't have survived even if he were in the hospital when it happened. I went ahead and moved here because this is where I feel the closest to my Jack; this was our dream, to live together here." She wiped copious tears from her eyes and face and sniffed into her hankie. "Sorry, dear. I can still feel it like it was yesterday, but it was all of three years ago."

"I lost my Grammy three years ago too. She was my best friend, other than my brother." Fern smiled sadly and empathetically, and we sat for a while in silence, lost in our respective memories. I thought that maybe some ghosts were not so bad to carry around with you, especially those of people you really loved.

After a few seconds, Fern perked up a little and said, "Well, how about that tea I promised you, dear?"

Chapter 11

Still

I didn't make it home until past dark that night, although darkness fell around 5:30 pm at that time of year, so it was probably still early in the evening. Spook escorted me to the edge of the woods but wouldn't come any further even though I tried to coax him. Just as well though. Who knows what my crazy family would do to my new friend. I told him I'd be back the next day and hoped he understood me so I could find him again.

As I crept past the shed, I noticed candlelight flickering long fingers of light through the cracks around the door. I knew from the occasional clink and clang that Irv was still in there building God-knows-what. I hoped he was building a rocket ship to take him far away from there. Maybe he'd even ask me to go along. But I was pretty sure it was probably some kind of distillery for making moonshine. I decided to stop in and check out his handiwork.

He jumped when I opened the door. With his back to me, he tried to hide his contraption behind his outstretched arms like I would know what it was by looking at it. It just looked like a bunch of tubes and pots and gadgets to me. He looked over his shoulder and when he realized it was me, he relaxed a little but still said rather curtly, "Hey, get outta here, okay? I don't want Dad to know what I'm doing."

"What *are* you doing?" I asked.

"It doesn't matter; just go, okay?"

"Okay…" I turned to leave but paused before going out. "Can't you at least tell me what it is? So I don't worry about you, you know."

Irv turned around slowly, obviously pondering what to say. At last he said simply, "Something to make life easier. Don't worry; it'll be okay. Now go."

"Still I'd like to know what you're doing."

"That's what it is."

"That's what *what* is?" Irv's shorthand dialog was getting tiring.

"A still. Now go."

"Oh…Yes, of course it is."

As I turned to leave, Irv growled, "Don't tell Dad." As if I ever would. Even though Dad used to call me Tattle Taylor, I never tattled on Irv. Or anyone for that matter. Even though I always had so much I could reveal about every one of them.

When I entered the house, I found it dark

and quiet. Everything seemed eerily still. In the living room, I was startled by a slight movement. It was Dad sitting in Uncle Owen's favorite armchair, staring through the moonlit darkness straight at me. He seemed to stare through me though, not really at me, and made no move to recognize my presence. I shivered slightly and instinctively went to Mom's room to check on her.

I opened the door to find her bony form lying on top of the covers of her bed. She was wearing her thin nightgown even though it was cold, and her face looked like porcelain in the moonlight. My heart and stomach clenched together. Had she died of the neglect she had inflicted upon herself? Had Dad done something to her?

"Mom?" My quivering voice was barely audible, but she heard me and tuned her head slowly to look at me. I nearly jumped out of my skin. The dark circles around her sunken eyes contrasted with the stark whiteness of her emaciated face, making her look exactly like a long-dead skull. She reached out a bony hand to me and I hesitated a moment before taking it.

"Mom?" I asked again. "Are you all right?"

"No," she said in barely a whisper and then said, more strongly, "Yes, I'm okay. I suppose Dad needs me to cook him something, right?"

"I don't know. I was just worried about you, Mom."

She smiled and begrudgingly sat up. "Thank you for always being so sweet. Don't worry about me though. I'm not worth the trouble." She stood and left me in the room, surrounded by my memories of the ever-constant fear of becoming an orphan.

I climbed the stairs to my room, wrapped myself in Aunt Helen's old hand-crocheted afghan, and cried for the first time in a long time.

Chapter 12

Close

In the morning as I was headed out the door, Dad stopped me. "Where's Irvine?" he demanded.

"I don't know; I just got up."

"Find him."

I checked Irv's room and the rest of the house even though I knew where he most likely was. I just didn't want Dad to know I knew. Also I didn't want to lead Dad to him, so I pretended to search around outside until I was sure Dad wasn't watching before heading to the shed where Irv was building his still. As I passed the hog pens, the hogs snorted angrily at me, grunting and squealing their anger at not having been fed yet. That was probably why Dad wanted Irv found; it was now his chore to feed the hogs every morning.

I found Irv curled up in his coat on a pile of rolled up carpet on the floor of the shed. Behind him, the still waited expectantly in a blizzard of dust floating in the sunlight streaming through the sole window. I shook Irv awake and told him Dad was looking for him. He jumped up, shaking the sleep off him as if the dust had settled on him like snow. He shot me a startled look, but I shook my head and assured him, "He doesn't know I came here."

All the same, he cracked the door open and looked in all directions before he slunk out, leaving me to my own discretion. I wandered back to the house by a circuitous route, planning my later escape to the woods as I walked head-down.

"Did you find him?" Dad startled me out of my wits.

"Yes."

"Where was he?" he asked.

"Uh…just walking around."

Dad eyed me suspiciously, then we both jumped as the hogs began squealing at Irv, who was carrying two buckets of feed toward the hog pen. Dad looked back at me again as if he was going to say something but then decided against it and walked away to the barn.

When I looked over at Irv, he was staring at me, his eyes widened from the panic of almost being caught. Then he smiled slightly and his eyes became hooded again as he shook his head and went back to his chore.

Later, Irv made one of his rare appearances in my bedroom. "Damn, it's cold up here, Taylor."

"I like it that way," I said.

"That was close today. You don't think Dad caught on about the…thing, do you?"

"He's suspicious, but no, I don't think he knows anything. Yet anyway." Irv nodded and turned to leave. "You know he'll find out sooner or later, right?"

Irv paused and sighed, his shoulders dropping in resignation. "Yeah, I know." He looked back at me. "I'm hoping to get my first batch made before he does though."

"How long will that take?"

"Should be ready in a week or two. Meanwhile I'm going to stay away from it. You should too."

"I will. I promise." I made a mental note to change my path to the woods so that I wouldn't have to walk by the shed.

Chapter 13

Christmas

I visited Fern several more times that month, Spook always pressed to my side like a distorted shadow of me. The more time I spent with Fern, the fonder I became of her, and I began to feel relaxed and safe in her little cabin. It was almost as if the spirit of Grammy filled the small space, protecting and loving me like she always had. I was sure it was she who had sent Spook to find me that day in the woods.

Fern began teaching me the old ways "to help me survive whatever comes," she said. I still hadn't told her just how difficult survival for me had been, but I appreciated the knowledge she shared so lovingly.

As I marked off my calendar one day back at home, I saw with some indifference that the next day was Christmas. Christmas had never held the same magic for me as for other children, who could always count on stockings full of treats and presents under a tree. I read about that kind of family life and occasionally we would get to experience it at Grammy's or a foster home if we were lucky enough to be there at Christmastime, but usually we were with Mom and Dad whose excuse was always that we couldn't afford any of that commercial nonsense. But I knew it was because they needed the money for their cigarettes and 'ice'.

Nevertheless, I decided if I couldn't celebrate with my family, I'd celebrate with my new friends, Spook and Fern. After all, Christmas was supposed to be about love, family, and Jesus, not about all the presents, and I was beginning to feel more a part of Fern's family than my own. I figured I could spare one of Grammy's hankies for Fern, just to show her how special she had become to me. Finding a gift for Spook was easy—anything to eat. I figured some of the butchered hog entrails would be perfect. I wondered if dogs could be contaminated with the ghosts of people but decided that the spirit of Grammy would protect him. I packaged my gifts with whatever leftover wrapping paper I could find in Aunt Helen's storage and stowed them in my pack along with some snacks for me and of course my field guides.

That morning, I left early before anyone was awake. I didn't want to chance the unlikely event that Irv or Mom or even Dad would realize it was Christmas and demand to spend time together. It was strange that something I had wanted my entire life now seemed repugnant to me; the circumstances we found ourselves in made every move toward a normal family life suspect and undesirable.

The morning was colder than it had been and I was glad that I had wrapped a blanket around me over my coat. As usual, Spook was waiting for me at the edge of the woods and was beside himself with joy when he saw me. I'm not sure if it was me or the aroma of hog entrails coming from my backpack that excited him so that day. I wondered where he went in between the times I was with him. How did he stay warm, where did he sleep at night, what did he eat? Did he wait here at the edge of the woods for me all night or did he come every morning just in case I showed up? However he did it, Spook was a survivor like me, and I felt we were perfect for each other.

We found Fern outside at her cabin, decorating a straggly pine tree in the yard with old glass ornaments and tinsel. She laughed merrily and invited us to help. I put my backpack in the house, and Fern showed me how to place the decorations on the tree. It's an art, you know, and one I had never had the chance to learn. Fern was incredulous that I had never decorated a tree before, and I think it added to her growing suspicions that my family life was not ideal, especially since I had chosen to spend Christmas with her instead of them.

After we finished the tree and stood back a few minutes admiring it, we went inside the cabin to warm up. The cabin was filled with the aroma of some kind of sweet bread baking. It was a smell I only remember from times I spent with Grammy. To my knowledge, Mom had never baked anything in her life, at least not while I'd known her.

Fern made pine needle tea, which she told me was high in vitamin C and perfect for boosting our immune systems. She pulled a loaf of cranberry bread from the Buck Stove oven. "I made it from a mix that Lauren brought me," Fern said. "I added some dried berries I harvested earlier in the year though." I had never tasted anything so delicious.

After breakfast, I gave Fern and Spook their gifts, and Fern gave me something almost as precious as the treasure from Grammy. Spook gobbled up his gift and then curled up for a nap by the stove. Fern handed me a book—*A Painted House* by John Grisham—and told me it was her favorite. "I want you to have it, dear. It was even autographed by the author. Jack and I met him once on a trip to Atlanta."

But that was not the precious gift; this was:

Fern smiled tenderly at me and said, "Dear girl, I thought I would be happy to live out the rest of my life here alone with my books and my memories, but I find myself yearning for your visits more and more. If you ever need a place to live, if things get rough at home or whatever happens, you will always be welcome here. There's not a whole lot of room, but there's the loft if you'd like some privacy."

I couldn't help the tears that spilled out of my eyes, but I smiled sadly and took both of Fern's hands in my own. "I would like nothing more," I said, barely above a whisper. "But Irv needs me to watch out for him. He's not well. Mom too. I worry about them."

"I understand, dear. But if anything changes, you know where you can come."

Somehow just the knowledge that I wasn't trapped with my family anymore, that at any moment I could just walk away and have a loving home to go to, made me warm inside.

When I got home that afternoon, Mom, Dad, and Irv were laughing and talking loudly. It was surreal and at first I thought I was in the wrong place, but soon I learned the reason they had awakened from their apathy: Irv's moonshine. The grain alcohol had made them giddy with joy at the end of their 'prohibition.' Mom and Dad danced around while Irv enjoyed being the center of their attention and affection. It seemed no one had even noticed I had been gone all day.

The warm feeling I had gotten from Fern chilled with the frosty air of my bedroom as I pulled the covers over my head.

Chapter 14

Snow and Ice

After a six-day binge, my family awoke from their stupor to find that not only was the alcohol all gone but also, in his oblivion Irv forgot to start a new batch of liquid salvation. Irv stewed, Mom cried, and Dad yelled. I tried to melt into the background. To make matters worse, Irv found that the quickly dropping temperatures had cracked some of the tubing on his still.

When Dad heard that, he went into a rage, pushing things off tables then overturning the tables themselves, throwing vases and other breakable objects at the wall, reveling in the sound and sight of destruction all around him. Things got really scary when Dad reached the kitchen and started throwing knives. One just missed Irv's head as it sunk into the door behind him. "Go make more juice!" he yelled.

While Irv was out in the shed, Dad turned his anger to me. He said he knew what I had been doing all those times I went into the woods alone—I was meeting a drug dealer and scoring some ice. I retreated to my room, but Dad soon followed. That's when he stormed into my room and broke my unicorn. It was the first time I really considered leaving my parents. But I knew I couldn't go without Irv. Somehow I had to talk him into leaving with me. I didn't know if Fern would be open to having two of us, but I had to figure something out.

The new year brought lots of snow and frigid temperatures. Some days it was so cold and the snow was so deep, I couldn't make it to Fern's. I worried about her and especially Spook, but Fern had told me on Christmas Day that Spook often came back to the cabin at night when it was cold. I could only hope that they were together helping each other to survive when I couldn't make it there.

Irv was frantic to fix his still. He brought it piece by piece into the house and reassembled it in the living room under Dad's close supervision. After combing the entire farm for parts to replace the cracked ones, to no avail, Dad gave Irv an ultimatum: fix the still or get out—more precisely, "get the hell out and don't come back."

Irv started preparing for a trip to town, gathering up supplies he could trade for the needed parts. I had to stop him from raiding our supply of canned food, instead talking him into taking some of the butchered pork.

"I'm coming with you," I said.

"No you're not."

"Yes I am," I said resolutely.

"You have to stay and take care of Mom. Dad's jonesing; I don't know what he'll do to her."

"Oh, so you don't care what he'll do to me though." I put my hands on my hips and stared him down.

Irv looked at me and shook his head. "Taylor, I haven't worried about you since we were little kids. You're the toughest, smartest, best survivor there is. Hell, you live in an ice box up there in your room and you don't even flinch when Dad yells at you. You really live up to the nickname Ice Queen, you know."

I tried to be mad about what Irv was saying, but the truth was it made me proud. Proud that my big brother had so much respect and belief in me that he felt he didn't have to worry about me. I certainly didn't feel the same way about him. I didn't know how long he was going to be able to survive under these conditions.

Chapter 15

Frozen

At the end of a three-day warm-up, during which most of the snow melted, Irv set out to town, leaving me behind supposedly to guard Mom. Instead, I immediately headed out to check on Fern and Spook.

They were fine, of course. Fern had been living without electricity for several years and thanks to Lauren and her husband John, who came every fall to cut and stack enough wood to last her through the worst of winters, Fern had been completely unaffected by PF Day. The cabin was warm and dry, and the small hand pump on the sink brought up fresh water from the well pipe that had been installed under the cabin, ensuring that it stayed unfrozen as long as the cabin was heated.

Fern had an attached storage shed full of canned and boxed food, and she occasionally fished and trapped small game to implement her food supply. That day she taught me how to make snares for small game, using wire and sticks. She taught me several different ways of making them, including ones in trees for squirrels and birds and ones on the ground for rabbits and other ground-dwelling game. When we had several made, we went outside where she showed me how and where to set them for the best chance of catching game. She explained that many snares had to be set in order to increase the odds of catching anything. After the snares were set, it was just a waiting game. She would check on them twice a day to see if we had been lucky.

When we went back inside to warm up with a cup of hot tea, Fern repeated the invitation for me to come stay with her. "I'd love to," I said, "but I can't come without Irv."

"Well, then bring him with you," she said, and I could tell she meant it. "It'll be nice to have a man around to do some of the work."

I went home early that day, my heart happy at the prospect of both Irv and me finally getting away from our oppressive home. I expected to welcome home Irv before dark, eager to tell him about Fern's offer, but the sun went down with no sign of him. The temperature plummeted and the patches of melted snow and ice froze up again. I hoped Irv had found a friend to stay with in town instead of trying to make his way home in the cold and dark. I filed my worry away inside my brain and slept soundly, worn out by the day's activities.

Early in the morning, a light snow began, its delicate flakes reflecting the meager sunrise, turning the view outside my window into an inside-out snow globe. I watched, mesmerized, for a long time until the snow quit and everything lay still and silent under the soft blanket of snow. I sat at my window all day, watching the road to town, waiting for my brother to return.

In the evening, it started to snow again, this time with more purpose; the clouds that had hung over us all day seemed determined to make the earth their mirror image. By the next morning, they had succeeded, with mounds of snow reminding me of big fluffy clouds as I looked down from my window on the land below.

Again I hoped Irv would stay put instead of trying to trek home in the shin-deep snow. I put my anxiety and my life on pause, waiting and watching for the return of my brother, much like Fern would be waiting and watching for a successful snare.

My life remained on pause for days as I waited for Irv to return. After two weeks of snow and bitter cold and no sign of my brother, I decided to go find him. The only problem was I had no snow boots and the snow was now up past my knees. I just made it to the end of the long driveway before I was exhausted, and my feet were wet and near frozen. I returned to my room and for the first time since Irv left, I cracked opened the cabinet of worry deep inside my brain just a little and let the ink stain of despair start to seep into my subconscious.

Two days later, a figure on a horse appeared on the horizon of the road about midday. At first, I was ecstatic, thinking Irv had found a way to get home through the snow. I ran down the stairs and out the front door, uncharacteristically shouting on the way, "Irv is home!" Mom and Dad followed me out.

By then the horse had made it to our driveway, and we could see right away that the rider wasn't Irv; it was the town's sheriff, Ian Donald. He was a familiar figure to our family, having gone to school with Mom as well as having arrested both Mom and Dad on occasion. Dad faded back into the doorway, no doubt planning his escape if necessary. Sheriff Donald dismounted and walked up to Mom, taking his fur-lined aviator hat off as he did. Mom stood frozen in fear. There was just nothing good that the sheriff could be coming all this way for. Were they coming to arrest Mom and Dad? Had Irv been arrested in town?

Sheriff Donald stood still, looking at the

ground for a moment that seemed to hang in the air like an icicle. Then he looked up at Mom in a way that made my blood turn to ice. His eyes were sad, so sad, and the sorrow went deep—I could see right through them to his soul; he didn't want to have to tell Mom why he had come. The words welled to the surface along with the tear that spilled out onto his cheek and seemed to freeze there.

"Libby..." he said and the word sounded like a sigh. Then he looked up at Dad in the doorway and started again, "Kyle, I'm so sorry..." Mom's shoulders started to shake as the sheriff looked back at her, this time reaching out for her hand and peering into her eyes. She seemed to sense what this was about—a mother's intuition, I guess. "We found Irvine in the park this morning, frozen..."

"No!" I screamed involuntarily, throwing my hands up to cover my ears. But it didn't help; it couldn't block the horrible words that kept coming, kept intruding on my brain, filling every crevice with the blackness that had started days before.

As I heard the words, "He's gone," the stain flooded my world with darkness, and I tumbled into the abyss of despair that had been threatening to take over my life since I was born.

Chapter 16
Black

Days and weeks followed of which I have very little recollection. I don't know how I survived the blackness. For the first time in my life, I knew exactly how Mom felt when the darkness descended upon her and hung over her like a never-ending storm. Everything seemed dark, even in the daytime, and there was a constant low rumbling in my ears that made me want to scream. I slept a lot and when I was awake, I covered my ears with my hands to try to block out the noise and the truth.

One of the few memories I have of that time was when I first awoke after passing out at the news of my brother's horrible death. I don't know how long I had been out or how long he had been there, but Dad was sitting in a chair beside my bed, his head in his hands. By now his beard had grown long and there was quite a bit of gray in it and the once black hair on his head. At first I didn't recognize him or my room or even who I was. There was a tiny moment of peace in the anonymity before the black overtook me, flooding my brain with all the dark memories that haunted me.

I must have made some sound or movement, maybe a clearing of my throat or a soft subconscious moan, because Dad sat up and looked at me. We stared at each other for several moments, neither of us wanting to start the unspeakable conversation. His eyes were red and his face pale, beyond his normal appearance of withdrawal symptoms.

He broke the silence by reaching beside his chair and bringing up a bowl of dry cereal, my favorite cornflakes, and a can of condensed milk, which he began to open with the hand-crank can opener. "You need to eat. Sit up," he said a little gruffly to mask his kindness. I turned away and stared at the window. "The sheriff said they found this in Irv's pocket. It's addressed to you." I turned and looked as Dad placed an envelope on my bed. I just stared at it, unable to move my limbs to retrieve it, as if I were frozen just like my brother.

Defeated, Dad set the food on my bedside table and went to the door. Halfway through the door, he stopped and said without turning around, "I didn't mean it when I said he couldn't come back. I really didn't." His voice cracked as he got choked up. "I'm sorry, Taylor." I knew he meant it since he called me by my real name.

Winter raged on like the torment in my head. I had stopped crossing off the days on my calendar when Irv died, so time slipped away without me knowing. I saw Mom very little during that time, both of us barely existing, preferring to sleep our lives away so we wouldn't have to face our reality. Dad kept us alive with food and water but couldn't bring us out of our depression.

I put Irv's letter with my most precious possessions in Grammy's shoebox, but I couldn't bring myself to read it yet. I felt I would die if I unlocked the agony Irv must have felt as he sat in that park, freezing to death. He always hated the cold. I couldn't force my mind to think about it, and my head constantly hurt as it cracked into shards of black ice trying to break up any coherent thought of his last days.

The winter faded into spring, though I barely noticed. My frozen brain began to melt into pools of black runoff, leaving me feeling mushy instead of frozen. Still I slept a lot, preferring the blackness of sleep to the blackness of reality. As the temperature of the world warmed, I still felt cold inside, however, I was hot on the outside, so I opened my windows and left them open through the nights, which were still chilly. The stench of the hogs was beginning to overpower the receding fresh air of winter, compounding my anguish. I slept most of the time with Grammy's perfume-spritzed hankie over my face to try to block out the smell of the animals and the despair.

One morning a heady aroma entered my brain before I was even awake. I know this because I was dreaming about a little purple fairy waving her tiny wand at the pools of darkness in my brain, turning each of them into a reflection of a fully bloomed lilac bush. For the first time in months, maybe years, I awoke with a smile, blissfully unaware of my misery for a few moments. As I lay there inhaling the scent of the newly bloomed lilac bush outside my window, the memories of my brother crept back in, although this time they were the good memories—the times we had spent with Grammy, the times he had taken care of me when we were young, the few times we had laughed together about something that now seemed so insignificant. I felt a small sliver of hope in my frozen heart, and I arose knowing that I was ready to read Irv's letter.

Chapter 17

Dear Taylor

As I read my brother's letter, I inhaled the scent of the lilacs to calm and fortify me. *Dear Taylor*, it began.

I know what you're thinking. Stop. I'm okay. I'm not suffering. I actually feel good. You were right about the cold. It numbs you and clears your head. You were right about so many things. You're the smartest and wisest person I've ever known. Also my best friend. Which is why I'm writing you, and only you, to explain things. No one else deserves to know. You're the only person I've ever trusted besides Grammy, and I'm happy to be seeing her again soon.

It made my heart warm to think of Grammy once again welcoming Irv into her loving arms.

Not that I'm mad at anybody. No-

body is to blame. Mom and Dad weren't the best parents, but they did what they could. At least they loved us in their own way. Kids at school, teachers, other people in town—they were all okay. Sure there was some meanness sometimes, but nothing I couldn't handle. Lots of people tried to help us, Bob and Lori, Uncle Owen, social workers, even some of our landlords. Some of my friends from school let me stay with them the past couple of weeks, even though they barely had enough food for their own family. They cared. They really cared. In the end though, whatever plagues my brain and Dad's and Mom's—hopefully not yours!—couldn't be helped.

I was heartened by the thought that Irv's friends and their families had cared for him in his last few days on earth.

You see, little sister, physical pain is nothing compared to the mental pain I was born with. Some of my very first memories are of sadness. I don't remember ever enjoying life. I don't remember playing much or singing or having friends. I know you haven't had many friends, but I remember you playing and signing to your stuffed monkey when you were little. Do you remember him? I think you named him Skippy. I don't know what happened to him though.

I smiled suddenly, remembering my floppy old friend Skippy. He had been old and worn already when I got him, but I loved him like he was my only friend. Which he kind of was when Irv was at school. He was one of the many casualties of a life of turmoil and constant change. I don't even remember when I lost him, but it was before I started school anyway.

I remember you getting excited when I brought new library books home for you to read. I always picked out books you would like, not ones I liked. Reading never held the magic for me that it did for you. The only thing that made me a little bit happy was to see you smile.

I never knew my brother had actually been thinking of me—ever. It seemed I was always the one looking out for him. When I thought about the books he had brought home, it became clear to me that he had picked them out for me, not for him. There were books about animals, science, and girl protagonists—none of which were things Irv gravitated towards. It was nice to find out that even though he never boasted about it, he had worried about me and wanted me to be happy.

I know my death won't make you happy. There's just no way around that. I'm sorry. I've come to realize that my life is not really a life at all and it has nothing to do with Mom and Dad or PF Day or anything else except me. You'll be better off without me, I'm sure. I've been an anchor around your neck for the past few years, keeping you from getting away and finding happiness. I know happiness is out there for you. You have a good soul, not a messed up one like mine and our parents'. Without me holding you back, you can do whatever it takes to get out of this miserable life.

Grammy's words about the diamond echoed in my head as tears filled my eyes. "Save it for when you're old enough to escape." Even though the thought of Irv being an anchor was excruciating and untrue, I understood what he meant; I had stayed longer than I should have because of him. I could have been living with Fern since Christmas, finding joy and comfort in life, if I hadn't been so concerned about Irv. Still, he couldn't have been more wrong; I had worked out how to save us both. I'd give any amount of future happiness just to have him back. Now I wasn't sure if I could ever be happy without him. His pain didn't go away, it simply transferred to me. It seemed that even though my heart was thawing, it was leaving behind a big hole where concern for Irv used to reside.

I don't mean suicide for you. It's the right way out for me, but not for you. And I don't just say that because I'm your brother and I love you. You have hope in you, a gift that you need to share with the world. You kept me going all this time with that hope. You kept our whole family going just by being you and you didn't even know it.

Hope. Did I have hope? If so, what was it?

You got to hold on to that hope, Taylor. You got to go out and find some happiness. You're never going to find it with Mom and Dad. They're unfixable, just like me. When I left, I told you to watch out for Mom, but I know now I shouldn't have. Sitting here in the cold has made me see that Mom will never get better and neither will Dad. Not without drugs anyway. It just seems so hopeless. Even when the electricity comes back on, what kind of life is it to have to be drunk or high or medicated into a zombie to keep you from wanting to end your life? To have no hope other than to score your next hit. I don't want that kind of life anymore, but there's no other one available to me. It was the way I was born.

I realized that even when I felt the lowest and darkest after Irv's death, I never wanted to end my life. Maybe that was the hope he was talking about. Maybe he was right. Maybe he had been the smart one all along.

But not you, Taylor. Your brain works different. Thank God! You've got to get away before it's too late. Find someone in town to live with or go live with the lady in the woods.

I didn't remember ever telling Irv about Fern. Maybe he had followed me once to make sure I was okay. My heart warmed again at the thought that he had cared enough to find out where I was going all those times.

Make something of your life. Don't waste it like the rest of your family whose only concern is scoring some ice. Find a good boy to love, raise a family, love them like Grammy loved us. As I leave this world, I have more hope than I've ever had, but now my hope lies in you and your future. I'm happy that my pain is coming to an end and that now you can begin to really live life. I love you, Taylor.

Your big bro, Irv

As I placed the letter back in its envelope and then back in the shoebox, I suddenly knew what I had to do.

Chapter 18

Escape

As I gathered my few belongings to move to Fern's cabin, I briefly wondered what I would do if she hadn't survived the winter, as unlikely as that seemed given her amazing survival skills. Still, she was an old woman, probably in her late seventies at least, and you never know what might happen. I decided that even if she had died, as sorrowful as that would be, I'd still move in to her cabin and honor her memory by trying to make it own my own for a while. Hopefully Spook would be there to help me.

When I went downstairs, I found Dad and Mom in good spirits. I was mystified until I discovered the source of their excitement. Dad was about ready to "harvest" a new batch of hooch that he had brewed up in the still, which he had moved to a shed outside.

I took Mom's hand and led her into her room, ostensibly to "talk about girl stuff." Once inside, I closed the door and sat beside her on the bed. She smelled of grief and decay despite her excitement about the imminent fix of alcohol.

"Mom, I'm leaving. I can't stay here anymore."

Mom's simulated smile melted, and the sadness crept back into her eyes. "I always knew this day would come." A tear slipped out of her eye.

"I'll come back and visit. I promise."

"I know," she said, but the look in her eyes said she didn't really believe it. She took my hands in hers and stared at me for a few moments. "Taylor, I've wanted for so long to say…" She sniffed and looked down, withdrawing her hands to her lap at the same time. "I've wanted to tell you that I'm sorry. I'm sorry we weren't better parents to you and Ir—," she choked on his name, "your brother." She paused to wipe her tears and her nose. It was the most emotion I'd seen from her in years. "Having you two was the only good thing I ever did in my life. Things would have been different if I hadn't met your father. Your real father, I mean. Sometimes I wish I had never met him…" Her voice trailed off with her thoughts.

"But then I wouldn't have had you," she continued with renewed conviction. "You are the only bright spot in my life."

"Mom, I didn't think you even knew I was here most of the time," I gently admonished.

"I know. I know it probably seemed that way. But honey, you were always on my mind. It's just that sometimes… Sometimes I wasn't able to show it." She looked down again. "I have a little drug problem, you know." Understatement of the century, I thought. "But I wasn't always like that. I took good care of Irv when he was a baby. Well, as good as I could, what with trying to protect him and avoid being hit by that good-for-nothing son-of-a-bitch that fathered you.

"I left him as soon as I found out I was pregnant with you. I just couldn't bear the thought of subjecting another baby to his abuse. And it was getting worse. I was scared he would make me lose you. The problem was I didn't have anywhere to go, so I ended up shacking up with a nice guy who turned out to be a drug dealer. He was okay but he was more concerned with his 'business' than he was with having a family.

"After I had you, I had the worst case of the baby blues. Al—that's the drug dealer—introduced me to some drugs that helped me feel better. That's all it took. Now I'm hooked and I can't seem to ever feel good unless I have some kind of ice.

"Anyway, that's when I met your Dad. He was a user too, but he really cared for us, so I moved in with him. I've never regretted that even though things haven't turned out like I wish they had. Especially with Irv." She started sobbing then, and I took her in my arms to comfort her, our roles reversed yet again. I told her goodbye then, comforted by the thought that she'd soon escape to alcoholic euphoria so she could forget about the losses of her life for a while.

Deciding not to say anything to Dad, I picked up my duffel bag of belongings I had left at the bottom of the stairs and started to head out. At the last minute, I stopped by Irv's room. Something drew me in, like a whisper from beyond. Maybe it was Irv's ghost, but I wasn't afraid. Like Grammy's spirit, I could never be afraid of Irv's ghost, especially now that I knew he was at peace. I moved around the room, picking up the few belongings he had clung to, trying to figure out if each was what Irv wanted me to find. In one of his nearly empty dresser drawers, I found a journal and I was surprised to see that Irv had been writing in it. Not for very long, obviously, but for the past few months at least. I knew in my heart that this was what Irv wanted me to find and I stuffed it into my bag to take with me.

I felt that a weight was beginning to lift from me as I held my breath past the hog pens, the old black hog snorting a goodbye as if he knew I wouldn't be coming back soon. A small sliver of hope in my brain supported his expectation.

Chapter 19

Home

I didn't expect Spook to be waiting for me after all this time, but he was. He was even more delighted than I was at our reunion. He kept jumping and twisting, rubbing against my jeans, licking my hands, making me giggle with his enthusiasm. It felt like I was starting my journey home.

As I neared the cabin, I was overjoyed to see Fern alive and working in her raised garden beds behind the cabin. The soil was still barren after the long cold winter, and she was turning it with a shovel, preparing it for planting. It was backbreaking work, especially for someone as old as Fern, but she was spry and could work circles around most people younger than she.

Amid Spook running and barking around us, Fern enveloped me in her strong arms, her welcoming smile as warm as the sun shining overhead.

"I wondered if we'd ever see you again, dear!" she said, hugging me again. "What kept you away? Your family? Is everything all right?" At the look of sadness in my eyes, she pulled back and assessed the situation of me with my duffel bag but no Irv. "Your brother. Did something happen to him, dear?"

I was amazed at the shrewdness of this woman; no wonder she had survived so long. "Yes…" My voice dropped to a whisper. "He died in January.

"Oh, my dear sweet girl." Fern pulled me back into her arms, this time stroking my hair as she talked. "I knew it had to have been something bad for you to come here to stay without him. Come inside and have some tea, dear. You look like a skeleton. How long's it been since you've eaten?"

We went inside where Fern plied me with food and tea while I told her everything. I even poured out the ugly truth about my family and their addictions. I figured if I was going to live with Fern, I shouldn't keep secrets from her, especially since Mom or Dad might just show up on our doorstep one day. Besides, it was cathartic to get it off my chest. That night I slept peacefully in the loft with the window open to the cool night air.

The next day, Fern filled me in on all that had happened since I was last there, which wasn't much. She was excited to tell me that some of the snares I had set were successful and that she had had plenty of rabbit and squirrel to supplement her canned foods, smoked fish, vegetables from her root cellar, and dried berries. She had even tanned three of the rabbit skins, making them into warm winter hats for us. She didn't have to explain that the third had been meant for Irv. She showed me how she had smoked and dehydrated some of the meat in a small smokehouse out back. She said she was eager to get down to the river to start catching fish to eat and smoke. When I told her I'd never gone fishing, she 'tsked' and said I was in for a treat.

We went fishing a few days later when Fern deemed it was warm enough. We took a picnic lunch and stayed all afternoon and into the evening. It was relaxing and peaceful, even with the excitement of landing a few fish. The aromas of grass, moss, water, and especially fish permeated my senses. At first the fishy odor bothered me but after a while, it became comforting, reminding me of the times Grammy had made catfish for dinner.

I especially loved sitting on the bank listening to the metallic gick-gick-gick of breeding cricket frogs after sunset. Fern said we would be able to catch bullfrogs in a couple of months and that their legs taste "just like chicken." She identified all the different animal sounds around us. I never realized nature could be so noisy and so peaceful at the same time.

We walked slowly home up the trail through the woods, while Spook chased fire-flies ahead of us. It had been a beautiful day that would repeat itself many times that summer, just one of the many reasons I finally felt at home.

Chapter 20

Power

Early one morning in June, we awoke to the sound of a truck outside the cabin. We nearly jumped out of our skins, so alien was the sound. Nevertheless, we threw on our clothes and went outside to see who was invading our Eden. Fern was delighted to see Lauren and John Powell driving an ancient pickup truck. I was happy to see them too, but I was a little worried that they'd tell the authorities where I was.

Lauren sat and talked with us as John quietly went about unloading the pickup. She was as animated and outgoing as her husband was calm and unobtrusive. A perfect fit, I thought. They had brought us a chicken coop with one rooster, three laying hens, and twelve chicks. Lauren explained that since PF Day there had been no canned food manufactured to replenish Fern's pantry, so they brought live food instead. They also had some home-canned food, but it wouldn't be enough to last us through the next winter.

The next thing Lauren said astonished us.

"Now that the power is back on, maybe we'll be able to buy food for you before winter."

The power was on. It hadn't occurred to us that it was a possibility, or even a concern to us for that matter. I wondered if Mom and Dad had power now, and if they would stay on the farm to await justice or decide to try to stay ahead of the law. Hopefully they wouldn't find us out here in the woods and force us to give them sanctuary.

At one point, Lauren pulled me aside and said gently, "Taylor, we're so sorry about Irvine. We heard about it in town before we came here." She pulled me into a hug. It seemed lots of people other than my family liked to hug me, and I was beginning to like it. It felt like I was a part of 'normal.' She continued, "How are your Mom and Dad?" When I murmured that they were okay, she added, "If you ever need anything, Taylor—food, clothes, a place to stay, anything—you are always welcome in our home. Remember that, okay?" My head was dizzy with the thought of being able to be a part of my dream family.

The Powell's left with promises to return after the harvest to replenish the firewood supply and bring more food. Fern hugged them and said, "You are so good to me. What did I ever do to deserve wonderful friends like you? How can I ever repay you?"

To which Lauren replied, "We can never repay you for the wonderful friendship and care you gave Grandma. But I'd come to see you just because you're you and I love you, Fern." They both had tears as they hugged goodbye. Even John hugged Fern as Lauren hugged me. And then they were off in the rattletrap truck, apparently one of the few vehicles that survived the sun's assault on PF Day.

The lovely days of spring rolled into hot and humid summer days, filled with satisfying chores and invaluable lessons in survival. We tended the garden beds, first planting and then checking on them every day to ensure the most successful harvest. Fern planted by the 'square foot' method instead of by rows so there were hardly any weeds to pull. She explained how she and her dear late husband, Jack, had improved the concept by combining it with another gardening concept called hugelkultur, which helped to ensure that the beds stayed moist during droughts. They first dug two or three feet down into the ground and placed rotted wood, branches, and small trees into the trenches, which would hold moisture and add nutrients to the soil, then built the raised beds on top. They also added pipes coming directly from the well that Fern could open in extremely dry weather to automatically water the beds. The combination was an ingenious way to amplify the harvest with a minimal amount of work.

Fern showed me the small root cellar that Jack had dug into a small hill near the cabin. It went down twelve steps and opened up into a room about ten feet square, lined with shelves and bins for storing harvested vegetables and some fruits such as apples. I loved the earthy smell of dirt and drying vegetables. The temperature was markedly cooler in the cellar. Fern said it stayed about 50°F year-round. It wasn't cool enough for actual refrigeration, but she said that in the old days, people would cut huge chunks of ice from frozen rivers or ponds, wrap them in straw and sawdust, and store them in the cellars. The ice blocks would last most of the summer, providing not only refrigeration, but also ice for things like lemonade and making ice cream.

I was amazed at the cleverness of people in the old days and somewhat sad that most of that knowledge had not been passed down to modern society. Fern said often as she was teaching me the old ways combined with some new methods of survival, "Remember, dear, knowledge is power. And even more important, knowledge is the key to survival. As you can see, canned food will run out and without the knowledge to find and grow food, long-term survival is nearly impossible."

I realized how lucky my family had been to have Uncle Owen's farm to go to and how we had lived primarily on Aunt Helen's home canned food. If Mom and Dad decided to stay there, they were going to be in trouble soon though, when that food and the grain to feed the hogs ran out, because they didn't have the knowledge nor the drive to grow more. I hoped that since the power was back on, manufacturing and commercial agriculture would soon pick up to feed the starving, technology-dependent people of the world.

I thought it ironic that the people we used to think were backwards, the indigenous tribes and the poor of third world countries who lived without electricity, had probably fared better than the 'civilized' people. I also thought about all the useless 'knowledge' we learned in school and the wasted time we spent learning it. If knowledge is power, then certainly it should be the right kind of knowledge to help one survive in any situation.

Chapter 21

Harvest

The heat and cloying odor of summer melted into autumn, the cool crisp air invigorating both Fern and me. While we had enjoyed the lazy days at the river and nights sleeping under the stars on the verandah of the cabin, we looked forward to harvesting our gardens and processing the yield, canning some, dehydrating or storing others. There was so much to learn and I was more eager than ever to soak it all in.

Besides harvesting food from our gardens, there were lots of wild herbs and greens such as dandelion and purslane, mushrooms, berries, and medicinal plants to find and process. We had been smoking fish and small game we had snared all summer, and we had collected wild berries as they ripened. There were also several fruit trees on the property—apple, peach, and pear—as well as blueberry and gooseberry bushes to gather fruit from at different times throughout the summer and fall. We had butchered a couple of cockerels—young roosters—a nasty, smelly process, and collected eggs from our hens, being careful to leave a few to hatch new chickens to replenish our stock.

Fern said she had been rather lazy, not doing much home canning since Lauren had been bringing her manufactured canned foods, but now we would have to can as much as we could in case Lauren couldn't get enough for us. It was much easier with two people and now that she had me, she was eager to get started.

The canning process was hot and tedious, but it helped that we were able to do it on a stone wood-burning grill that Jack had built outside instead of heating up the cabin. After cleaning and cutting up the fruits or vegetables, they were cooked with seasonings in a pot on the grill. Then the cooked food was sealed into clean Mason jars, which were then sealed and boiled in a special canning pot full of water for a specified amount of time, depending on the food. Fern had a book that told the times as well as many recipes. She cautioned that if not done properly, bacteria like deadly botulism spores could grow in the jars and poison us. I was careful to pay special attention to the process. It would be such a cruel irony to have survived this long only to die from something we had done to ensure our continued survival.

We harvested and canned, dehydrated, and

stored food in the cellar for several weeks. By the end of September, we felt confident that we had enough food for a family of four to survive comfortably until spring.

On October 12th, Fern, Spook, and I were sitting in the rockers on the front porch, relaxing at the end of another fruitful day when we noticed the sky glowing after sunset. As the darkness of night enveloped us, the eerie glow in the north pulsated and danced, signaling the arrival of yet another coronal mass ejection, or CME. As Fern and I watched the beautiful spectacle, we couldn't help but wonder how it would affect the world. Would it destroy what was left of the crippled power grid? How would people survive this time? The Aurora was visible for several nights in a row, so we thought it must have been another big one.

Our answer came a few weeks later in the form of Lauren and John along with their youngest son, Calvin, who I knew from school, although this time they rode in a horse-drawn wagon. They confirmed that a second CME had reached the earth, again collapsing the power grid and that this time there was little hope of power being restored in the foreseeable future. They couldn't stay long though, because they were still trying to harvest what they could on their farm in the old way with a horse-drawn reaper.

They didn't have much in the way of canned food for us, but they brought grain for the chickens, smoked beef and pork, flour, and honey for us, and some other essentials like homemade candles and soap that they had bartered for in town. Lauren looked quizzically at me when I asked where they had gotten the pork—I wanted to be sure Uncle Owen's ghost wouldn't inadvertently be allowed into our sanctuary—but she assured me that they had traded beef to their neighbor for it. Fern insisted that Lauren take some of her dried medicinal herbs "for their trouble."

While John cut firewood, Calvin and I hauled it back to the cabin and stacked it in an oddly specific manner that Calvin insisted upon. When I asked about it, he explained that it was important to stack it in a way that the wood could dry and season correctly. I always knew that Calvin was smart—he and I were always vying for the top spot in the class grade rankings—but that day he impressed me with his knowledge of survival techniques to add to those that Fern had already taught me. He told me about a washing machine of sorts he had helped make for his mother out of some buckets and an oar, as well as a bicycle-powered grinding mill for making flour from grain, and solar lights made from soda bottles. He said he would be happy to come back after the harvest and help me implement some of these ideas to help Fern and me with our chores.

After they had left, my brain was in overdrive. Calvin had made me start thinking about ways to automate some of the more mundane or time-consuming chores such as laundry, which we had been doing by hand in the big wash basin in the cabin, and processing the harvest. I started making plans in my head to create some of my ideas through the winter months.

Another thing kept bothering my brain after their visit, and it had nothing to do with harvest or plans or survival, and everything to do with Calvin.

Chapter 22

Need

In early December, after weeks of thinking about, of all things, a certain boy, I decided we needed some supplies from town so I could work on my inventions. Fern was all for it, perceptively guessing my real reason for going when I mentioned that I might have to go on over to the Powell farm to get what I need.

"Yes, yes," she said with a wink. "Go get what you need, dear." I'm sure I blushed because she grinned and shook her head. "Ah, to be young again…"

I decided I'd better check on Mom and Dad if they were still on the farm, so I left early in the morning to stop by there. Spook walked me to the edge of the woods as usual and then stopped. As much as I wanted a companion for the trip, I was concerned how the townspeople would view him—as a pest or meat, maybe—so I decided to leave him to protect Fern and take my chances alone.

I found Dad tending the hogs, and he barely acknowledged me as I went by, just a nod in my direction so I knew he had seen me. I couldn't tell by his haunted eyes if he even registered that I had been gone for six months. Mom wasn't much better, but at least she hugged me limply and told me she missed me. The oppressive air clawed at my senses and the stench of the hogs made me gag. I couldn't wait to be on my way after making sure they had enough to survive, albeit not what they needed to be happy.

The walk to town was fraught with a mixed bag of emotions, mostly sadness and loneliness for my brother, but with some happy memories mixed in, and of course excitement about possibly seeing Calvin again. I was amazed when I realized that I hadn't thought much about Grammy and Irv while I was at Fern's. Maybe it was because I was usually busy there, or maybe because I felt so at home. Maybe it was that Grammy's and Irv's spirits were with me there, watching over me and making me feel loved all the time. Whatever it was, it was definitely not with me as I walked briskly along the deserted highway, feeling lonely and anxious.

In my backpack, I carried dried medicinal herbs and tinctures with instructions for their use, which Fern had made to trade for the items I needed for my inventions as well as some books, if I could get a hold of some. Fern was hungry for some new reading material since she had read the books in her library over and over. "Anything by John Grisham, please," she implored.

When I got to town just before noon, I was saddened to see some of the old buildings on the square burnt to the ground and others boarded up tight. The once manicured lawns of proud homeowners were overgrown and choked with the weeds of neglect, now a low priority for people struggling daily to survive. One bright spot, however, was Tipton's diner. It was open and several people were hanging around the front. One of the girls I knew at school, Jenny Garten, saw me and called me over.

"Hey Taylor, it's good to see you!" She threw her arms around my neck like we were long lost friends. Even though we really hadn't been, I enjoyed the idea. "Some of the kids are hanging out in back. You should come around with me." I agreed, thinking that Calvin just might be there against all the odds of a coincidence like that, since he lived a few miles the other way out of town.

Serendipity! For once that word belonged to me. There stood Calvin along with his brother Bracken, Skylar Tipton, the daughter of the restaurant owners, and several other kids from school. As I walked around the building, they all stopped talking and looked at me, and I realized that not only were they surprised to see me, they also were at a loss for what to say about Irv. After all, they had known about his death before I had.

Calvin was the one to break the silence and he sounded genuinely happy to see me. "Hi, Taylor!" After that, everyone said hi as Calvin pulled up a patio chair for me to sit in.

Bracken put his hand on my shoulder and said, "Hey, Taylor, we were all so sorry to hear about Irv. He didn't deserve that."

I wasn't sure how to answer, but I wanted them to know that at least for Irv, his death wasn't the worst thing that had happened to him. "It's okay," I said. "He's at peace now." They all nodded like they understood, and I'm sure they did; everyone in town knew about Irv's addictions.

Then the conversation moved to other topics, including sad news about other deaths and happy news about weddings and babies and such. In addition, the group was celebrating Calvin's fifteenth birthday, which had been two days before. Skylar brought out some food for all of us and insisted it was on the house when I tried to pay with some of the dried herbs I had brought to trade. She has always been such a sweet girl.

An hour later, I realized I would have to get to the square to make my trades if I was going to get back home before dark. I was reluctant to leave Calvin, but he decided to come with me, making some lame excuse about needing some supplies for some of his inventions. Ironic, right?

Chapter 23

Thunder

After an oddly enjoyable hour shopping with Calvin, I told him I'd have to hurry in order to get home before it was too dark out. The thought of walking the highway alone at night gave me the creeps even though there was not likely to be anybody else on the road. Calvin didn't like the idea either and said he had an idea. We went back to the diner to find his brother.

After a quick conference with Bracken, they insisted I allow them to take me home on their horses. Skylar volunteered to come as well. I was relieved for the chance to get home before dark and have companions along the way, but I eyed the horses with some trepidation. Even though I had spent most of my life in a town surrounded by farmland and chock full of schoolmates like Jenny Garten who owned horses, I had never been around the huge smelly beasts. Their manure and their sweaty hides assaulted my nostrils, although not nearly as bad as the same sources from the hogs. Still,

I couldn't help but feel a thrill of excitement about sitting atop one of them with my arms around Calvin. I admonished my brain to stop thinking these crazy thoughts; I didn't need a boyfriend—I was only thirteen after all.

Wait, was I just thirteen? I realized I missed a birthday somewhere in there. February 12th was the day of my birth, but my parents only occasionally recognized it as a special day. That year, I didn't blame them even minutely for forgetting though, as it was right after Irv left our world, and none of us were in the mood for celebrating anything, let alone an anniversary of coming into the world. Nonetheless, I smiled to myself, recognizing I'd survived to fourteen and was now only two months away from fif-teen.

The ride home was thrilling. The pounding of the horses' hooves, the nearness of Calvin as I clung to his back, the camaraderie of the four us enjoying our youth—all these things were as new to me as the happiness that had settled over my life. My heart soared with the hope that Irv was sure I had had all along. We made it to the hog farm in less than half the time it would've taken me to walk. I told Calvin to take me there and to not mention to anybody that I lived with Fern in the woods. Not that I didn't trust Bracken and Skylar, but you never know when something might accidentally slip out. The fewer people who knew, the better.

As we came galloping up to the house, the horses' hooves sounding like thunder from a gathering storm, Dad suddenly appeared on the porch with a shotgun pointed at us, yelling, "Get the hell off my property or I'll blow you away."

The boys reined in the horses immediately and I slid off from behind Calvin, telling Dad that it was okay, it was just me. "Fine," he said to me then turned back to the others. "Now get out of here like I said." To punctuate his demand, he shot a round into the air over the horses' heads. It was all Bracken and Calvin could do to get the horses back under control before turning them to leave.

Before kicking his horse to gallop away though, Calvin looked down at me and asked, "You going to be okay?"

I smiled at him wanly and said, "Sure. Thanks for the ride."

By the time the horses had left the yard, Dad had gone back inside. I skirted the house and instead of going in, headed for the woods. I was seething at the way Dad had treated my friends, and I was determined to not even stop in to talk to him or Mom.

Spook was waiting for me at the edge of the

woods to escort me home. We made it there just before sunset, and I was satisfied to see Fern waiting on the porch for me. Her relief and loving embrace made up for the cold shoulder I had gotten from my parents earlier.

Chapter 24
Secrets

The most exciting things Calvin and I found at the town market were two old CB radios. They had been stuffed away in an old metal military footlocker in someone's basement, and not knowing what to do with them, the owner sold them to us for some smoked ham that Calvin had brought to trade, along with some of the medicinal herbs that I had brought. Calvin said that they had probably been protected from the CME by the metal locker and that he was sure he could get them to work again.

We made plans for Calvin to ride over to the cabin with a manufactured excuse of some sort the next week. He promised to have both radios working by then. For some reason, without even conferring on it, we both wanted to keep our budding relationship a secret. We knew we couldn't keep it from Fern though, nor did I want to. She was unlikely to tell anyone, and I know she didn't disapprove. Anyway, she had already guessed it before I went to town, keen observer that she was.

After an excruciatingly slow week, Calvin finally showed up on the appointed day with the working CB radios and the buckets and oar I had needed to make an off-grid clothes washing machine. He said he was going to make it for me but decided I might enjoy making it together. It seemed he already understood me better than most people.

He had told his parents that Fern needed the washing machine and that he would be home before dark. He didn't want to lie to his parents about where he was going in case there was some sort of emergency. I admired that about him but also that his parents cared enough to want to know. Mine never did. I suspected that Lauren and possibly even John would guess the real reason of Calvin's visit, but he said they never mentioned it.

We spent the afternoon building the washing machine and going over some plans I had come up with for some inventions. Calvin seemed impressed and had some ingenious suggestions to improve them. We made a list of materials I would need and discussed how I could get them.

When it was time for Calvin to leave, I walked with him leading his horse up the old road to the highway, bypassing the hog farm altogether. We stood and talked on the shoulder of the highway for several minutes before the sinking sun forced him to leave. Just before he mounted his horse, he took my hand and stared into my eyes.

"Taylor, I'm glad we met again. I really enjoy spending time with you. Nobody else gets the way my brain works."

"I know what you mean," I said with a silly giggle. I was suddenly and inexplicably shy.

"Anyway, thanks for being my—" he paused, trying to figure out what we were to each other at that point. In the end, he decided to play it safe, "my friend."

I smiled and froze as he leaned his head closer for a quick kiss on my cheek. I could feel my cheek burning both from the excitement of the brush of his lips and from embarrassment, since I had never been kissed by a boy and I didn't know what I should do next.

I didn't need to worry though, because Calvin jumped up on his horse, said goodbye, and galloped off.

Chapter 25

Preparations

Weeks passed before I saw Calvin again. We stayed in touch with the CB radios, talking every night around midnight when Fern and most of the members of Calvin's household were asleep. Right before Christmas, Calvin told me that some soldiers had visited their farm, checking for radiation from the CME and warning about marauders that were terrorizing people in the area, particularly those on farms without close neighbors. It was sweet when he said was worried about us, but I didn't think anyone could find us back in the woods like we were. But still, I had an uneasy feeling and decided to keep Grammy's pistol loaded and nearby just in case.

When I took the gun out of its hiding place in the loft, I rediscovered Irv's journal that I had stowed away with all my treasures when I first came to live with Fern. After much emotional vacillation, I decided I was ready to read it. After reading the first page though, I wasn't so sure. The pain and anguish that Irv had poured out on those pages in his simple, concise manner were almost more than I could bear. Each phrase gave life to the feelings he had kept buried within him and hidden from those who loved him. If he had only told someone, Grammy or the school counselor maybe, they might have been able to get him some help. At least before PF Day, the day that made helping other people virtually obsolete. I could only read the first couple of entries before I put it away.

The next day I told Fern about what Calvin had said about marauders. She agreed that we should be extra vigilant even though it was unlikely that anyone would find us in the woods. Still, there was the old gravel road coming off the highway and leading almost to the cabin, which anyone might choose to follow. We were both glad to have Spook guarding our front door, either outside on warm nights or just inside the door on cold ones.

I showed Fern how to use the washing machine, although I told her I would do the washing most of the time. We didn't have much to wash since we didn't change our clothes as often as people did before PF Day. The biggest challenge was after we had run out of toilet paper and had to use pieces of cloth instead. In the summer, we gathered and used the soft leaves of the lamb's ear plant, but in winter they weren't available.

During the short days of winter, I worked on my inventions, first of which was a gravity-powered light so Fern would have something better than candlelight to read her new books by in the evenings. She had been rubbing her eyes a lot, and I concluded that the strain of trying to see in the dim light was bothering her. I had read about the idea in a science magazine at school the year before. It's a simple concept, using parts from an old microwave or other electronic devices. The trick was to find parts that had not been tied to the power grid on PF Day, because all those were fried by the sun's smack down. After playing around with it for a few days, I finally got my gravity light working, to Fern's amazement and delight. I gave it to her for Christmas, and she showered me and Spook with love and delicious food.

Another invention I worked on that winter was one that we wouldn't use for several months, a solar-powered fan made out of parts from an old computer to help cool the cabin in the summer. I also had plans to make a solar heat producer to help heat the cabin in the winter so we wouldn't have to burn so much wood, thereby reducing Fern's coughing, but I had no way to get the needed materials to the cabin.

Calvin said he would try to find the large sheet of glass, plywood and other pieces of wood, black paint, and empty aluminum cans I needed and deliver them with the horse and wagon. I didn't know how we could repay him for the materials and his time, but he said his parents would insist he do it for us for free anyway, so not to worry about it.

Calvin and I also talked about some ideas for defending our homestead against marauders. We agreed that Spook was the best defense we had at the moment, but what if something happened to him? I told Calvin about Grammy's gun but when I admitted I didn't know how to use it, he was adamant that he needed to come over and show me how.

Chapter 26

Invasion

As the nights grew longer and colder after the winter solstice, Spook wanted to stay in the cabin at night more often than not. He wasn't happy about it though, as he couldn't guard the property as well, and he got overheated when he slept downstairs by the front door, which was too close to the Buck stove. I began taking him into the loft with me and sleeping with the window cracked open, as much for my comfort as his. This made him somewhat happier, both because he could sleep by me and because he could see and smell a little of what was going on outside. Still, it made him nervous to be cooped up and not be able to patrol the homestead as he usually did at night.

One night after Calvin and I had talked on the CB radios and I had just blown out the candle by my bedside, Spook jerked to attention and started a low growl at something outside the window. I tried to see what it was that had gotten his attention, but there was very little light coming from a new moon. The hair on both our necks stood up as a dim, man-shaped shadow passed by in the yard and disappeared into the trees. I grabbed the gun and pointed it out the window, my hands shaking like an addict in withdrawal as the adrenaline coursed through my veins. After several minutes of no further movement, we calmed down a bit, but had trouble going to sleep for hours afterwards.

The same scenario played out for several nights in a row, until I started to think it was a strange recurring dream or some kind of dementia. For a while I though that maybe the mental illness that haunted Dad had come to roost in my brain, making me have paranoid delusions of ghosts invading our sanctuary. But Spook's reaction was all too real, and I didn't think a dog could share a mental illness with its human companion. So I didn't take any chances, keeping the gun at my side and being careful not to stand in front of the window when the candle was lit. In fact, I tried not to light the candle at all; I felt safer in the dark so no one on the outside could see me.

I didn't mention our ghostly visitor to Calvin because I didn't want him to worry nor did I want him to think I was crazy. I didn't tell Fern for the same reasons, although I knew at some point I might have to. Every night before bed, I checked the locks on the doors and windows to make sure no one could easily get in, and Spook and I remained on high alert for a couple of weeks.

The strain began to show, and Fern noticed how tired both Spook and I were in the daytime. At first she thought we were both sick but then figured out that we weren't sleeping. At her insistence, I finally told her about the ephemeral form that had been haunting us nightly.

In her usual straightforward, practical way, Fern insisted we confront the man—she refused to believe it was a ghost—and warn him away from our property, with the gun if need be. She knew how to load and shoot a gun, although she had never used this particular kind before. Nevertheless, after looking it over for a bit, she was able to load it, and we were ready to do some ghost-busting.

Chapter 27

Confrontation

On a dark and cloudy night in January, we slipped out the back door with Spook on a makeshift leash. We clung to the shadows of the wall as we watched for the intruder. After what seemed like hours of waiting, he showed up, and it was all I could do to keep Spook from growling or lunging. Fern immediately shined a big battery-powered spotlight, which she kept for emergencies, right into his face, at the same time yelling, "Stop! What are you doing trespassing in my yard?"

My heart clinched and I almost gasped audibly when I saw who it was. Dad. I pressed myself against the wall in the hopes he wouldn't notice I was there.

Dad shielded his eyes, trying to see who was spotlighting him. When he didn't answer, Fern yelled again with a strange accent, "I said whatcha doin' here? Answer or I'll shoot!" She moved her hand into the spotlight to show him the gun. She cocked it so he would know she was prepared to use it.

Dad put up both hands over his head and answered, "I'm just here looking for my daughter. Is she here? Who else is with you?"

Shrewd as Fern was, she knew not to expose me. Instead she said, "Me and my dog are out here, aren't we, Spook?" At the mention of his name, Spook stepped forward and growled a little at Dad. "My grown son's asleep in the house. Went to bed early with a headache. If I have to shoot this gun, it'll wake him up and, boy, will he be mad."

"What's your son's name?" Dad said suspiciously.

Without hesitation, Fern said, "I don't see as how that's any of your business, but his name is Jack and he's one mean and ornery cuss. You don't want to mess with him. He'd just as soon shoot you as talk to you. Now git off my property before I let my dog go and wake up Jack by shootin' at ya!" I could barely suppress a giggle at Fern's fake accent, which made her sound like an unfriendly hillbilly.

Dad wasn't similarly impressed but apparently decided it wasn't worth the trouble to put her words to the test. He simply turned and said over his shoulder, "Well, if you see a teenage girl, tell her her mother needs her." I gulped, wondering if what he said was true and what exactly it might mean. Then he said something that turned my heart to ice. "Tell her her good-for-nothing brother needs her too." As he walked off into the woods, headed toward the hog farm, he muttered, "That ought to get her attention."

I knew that Dad was not in his right mind at that point. Even though I was worried about my mother, I was sure that Dad wasn't telling the truth. Either that or he didn't know what the truth was anymore, as evidenced by the remark about Irv.

I was relieved that he was gone, but I had a feeling that it wouldn't be the last time Dad would haunt us.

Chapter 28

Solace

Calvin and I met several times in town that winter. He also rode his horse to our cabin a few times. The winter was unusually mild for our latitude, which made survival much easier and traveling more enjoyable. In town, we always met in the square, shopping the various booths for parts for our inventions. It was amazing to see the people of the town come together and help each other forge ahead in this new grid- and technology-free world.

On February 12th, Fern baked me a cake from a boxed cake mix that she had been saving in the food shed to celebrate my 15th birthday. She had arranged for Calvin to come over and surprise me. He brought me a beautiful bracelet that he had traded Skylar something for. Fern gave me a lilac seedling that she had dug up somewhere—I suspected the hog farm, but she wouldn't reveal her source—and had hidden in one of the cold frame garden beds. She said we would have to keep it in there until the soil warmed enough to plant it in a permanent place under the loft window so I could smell its fragrance every night in the spring. It was the best birthday I could ever remember.

By the end of February, we were finally able to gather all the materials for the solar heat exchanger, and Calvin delivered them to the cabin in the horse-drawn wagon. We put it together the same day, and the heat it produced on sunny days was enough to warm the cabin to 60°F without burning any wood in the Buck stove. We also made a solar water heater so water could be heated outside in the summer and we wouldn't have to use the stove to heat water in the tank that was attached to the stovepipe of the Buck Stove, thereby keeping the house much cooler.

In March, Fern and I made cold frames for some of the raised garden beds out of some old windows I traded for in town, so that we could start growing crops in early spring. Placing the windows on top of the garden beds allowed the sun to keep the young plants warm and protected from the still-chilly nights of March and April, extending our growing season by two months and increasing our yield accordingly.

In May, Calvin introduced me to a new boy in town. His name was Ben and he was an orphan from Kansas City. Calvin said he had lived with them for a couple of weeks but had decided that farm life wasn't for him and moved to town. He now lived with three college students, Doug, Dakota, and Matt, in an old abandoned Victorian house at the edge of town.

I liked Ben and talked to him often when Calvin had to do things with his parents in town. Ben had an underlying sadness to his eyes that no amount of laughter and camaraderie could disguise. All he would talk about, however, was the horrors of trying to find water, food, and shelter in the big city and how fortunate he was that his three friends had found and rescued him. He was obviously in awe of the guys and gushed gratitude when talking about them. They in turn treated him like their little brother, at times gently teasing him and at all times watching out for him. I felt a shard of ice in my heart every time I was around them, thinking of my big brother Irv, but I was happy that they gave some solace to poor Ben.

I had an overwhelming feeling that there was more to Ben's sadness than he told me. I was sure he had Post Traumatic Stress Disorder like lots of people in the United States and many parts of the world had now, but it just seemed there was something more. I surmised that his parents must be dead since he was with the guys instead of them, but he apparently didn't want to open up to me yet and talk about them. He kept saying he didn't want our friendship to be all about death and despair. We both had had enough of that.

Chapter 29

The Guys

During the summer, Calvin told me his mother wouldn't let him ride to town without someone going with him because of the growing threat of marauders, so that meant he couldn't come to the cabin at all without letting our secret out. He wasn't quite ready to do that and neither was I. In his absence I started daydreaming about him and silly things such as how nicely his blond hair contrasted with my dark hair and how he was the perfect height for hugging, even though we hadn't done that yet. I should have been thinking about how intelligent he was and how suited we were to each other intellectually, but no, biology overtook me that summer and I suddenly got all girly.

His travel restrictions also meant we couldn't meet in town weekly like we had been doing, but I still went on our allotted day just in case. On the days Calvin couldn't come, I usually found Ben and spent the afternoon with him. We became good friends although the sight of him didn't make butterflies in my stomach like Calvin did.

We spent most of the time hanging out in the 'secret laboratory' of the old Victorian house he shared with the three guys, who were engineering students and obviously extremely intelligent. At first they were reluctant to let me in on what they were doing, but when I told them about some of my inventions, they thought I might be able to contribute to their projects, which consisted of inventing and making things to help people survive. They made home defense systems, alternative powered appliances, and things that didn't need power but would be helpful to people.

Ben wasn't a genius like Calvin and the engineering students, but he was eager to learn and he took good notes for them. I enjoyed the camaraderie as much as the intellectual challenges. Matt was funny, and he and Doug were always throwing mock insults at each other. Dakota was more quiet and nurturing, somehow "mothering" all of us, making sure we had eaten and were drinking enough water. The three guys had beards, as did most of the men now, and Dakota was big and burly. It was amusing to see him hovering over us like a mother hen protecting her chicks. They made me feel like one of them instead of the only girl and just a teenager. I was comfortable there, feeling like these were 'my peeps' as the popular kids used to say in school.

Since it was summer, I was able to stay in town longer than in the winter since it stayed light until almost 9:30. I made it a point to check in on Mom on my way home from town each week, even though the odor of the diminishing herd of hogs made me gag. The strain of living was weighing heavily on her, and she looked more frail each time I saw her. I didn't think she was going to last much longer, but there was nothing I could do. I tried giving her herbs to boost her immunity and flush toxins from her body, but she'd push them away, saying, "It's no use, sweetie, I'm tired of living." I'd beg her to try to keep going, even resorting to tears at times, something I rarely did, but she'd just smile wanly, shake her head, and turn away, preferring to sleep what was left of her life away.

I couldn't avoid seeing Dad while I was there, but it was like he had become someone else. His eyes were constantly darting back and forth like he was seeing things all around him, and his lips were pressed together like he was afraid something might possess him through his mouth. Or maybe he was afraid to say something he'd regret either to me or to the unknown demons haunting him. In any case, he barely recognized that I was present and never answered when I asked him how he was.

I was always glad to leave, making sure I went back out to the highway and around to the gravel road instead of cutting through the woods like I used to. Spook would always be there waiting for me, and we would stand and listen for a time to make sure Dad hadn't followed me before heading down the gravel road.

As much as I enjoyed spending the afternoon in town, whether it was with Ben and the guys or Calvin, going home was always bittersweet because of the stopover at the hog farm.

Chapter 30

Harvest of Souls

In the fall as Fern and I began to harvest and process our summer bounty, I couldn't go to town for several weeks. I was surprised to find that I physically ached to see Calvin again but looked forward to seeing him after the harvest when he and his parents would come to help set us up for the winter. I was eager to show them all my inventions to help make us more self-sufficient although I didn't want them to think they didn't need to come anymore.

Fern and I had built a new large solar dehydrator and we were able to dehydrate three times as much meat, vegetables, and fruits as before, significantly cutting down on the amount we would need to can since our supply of new Mason jar lids to make a safe seal on the jars was getting low. Stored properly, dehydrated food will last six to twelve months without the threat of botulism or other food poisoning.

One day while I was outside preparing some vegetables for dehydrating and others for storing in the root cellar, Spook suddenly stood erect and started growling menacingly at the woods to the east, the direction of the hog farm. I instantly and instinctively knew that Dad had found me. Fern was in the root cellar and the gun was in the house. At a loss of what to do, I decided to try to talk to him.

"Dad, is that you?" I said. No reply, only a movement in the leaves. "Dad?" I said again, this time louder. I saw his haunted face among the leaves. "Come on out and talk to me." I forced my voice to sound calmer and more confident than I was feeling inside.

Finally he emerged, and Spook moved in front of me, still growling softly. "Hi Dad," I said. "How are you doing? How's Mom?"

He stopped and snorted with contempt. "Like you care," he growled, his wild eyes darting here and there, everywhere except at Spook and me.

"What do you mean?"

"You haven't come to see your Mom for weeks. You were the only one she wanted to see in the end." He spat out the words like a bad taste. My heart froze.

"What do you mean?" I said again, this time in little more than a whisper.

"She's dead, Ice Queen!" he yelled as he started shaking all over. I didn't know if it was from anger or sickness or grief, but it was frightening all the same. Spook moved toward him and started growling louder, baring his teeth to add extra warning. Dad didn't even seem to notice.

I started shaking as well, out of both grief and fear. This time something told me Dad wasn't lying, that Mom had truly passed and now her soul was free. Fleetingly, I thought of her ghost inhabiting Dad's vulnerable mind, but whether she would try to help him or haunt him, I couldn't decide.

All of a sudden Dad's wildly searching eyes focused on me and stopped, turning hard and evil as he stared into my soul. I almost fainted in fear as I stood frozen under his glare, and Spook prepared to lunge at him if he made any move toward me.

I don't know how long we stood like that, seconds probably although it seemed like millennia, but the spell was finally broken by Fern as she came around the house, Grammy's gun in her outstretched hands, pointed at Dad. "I tole you before to stay off my property," she said in her fake hillbilly accent. "I'd hate to have to shoot you and harvest your soul along with my vegetables." I was amazed at her fearlessness and confidence as she strode toward Dad, stopping halfway between him and me.

Dad's eyes unfocused again and quickly

went back to the wild darting. He didn't appear to be the least bit afraid of Fern, or Spook for that matter, but his hallucinations apparently began to close in on him and he put up his arms to shield his face, pressing his lips together and blowing air hard out through his nose. After several moments of flailing to fight off his invisible assailants, during which time both Fern and Spook looked at me questioningly, Dad turned and ran like he was being chased by a swarm of hornets.

It was only after he had disappeared into the woods and we couldn't hear him crashing through the underbrush, that all the emotions collapsed in on me and I sunk to the ground, shaking and crying. All the sorrow of losing my family, not only to death but also to their glacial descent into mental illness, hit me like an iceberg, and I felt my fragile heart shattering into pieces.

Chapter 31

Missing

It took several days of care and solace from Fern and Spook to repair my heart enough to resume daily life. I hadn't even felt like talking to Calvin, but Fern used the CB to get ahold of him and tell him what had happened. I felt bad that I had missed his 16th birthday, but he was much more concerned with my emotional well being than his birthday. Besides, he told me, it's not like he could get his license and drive a car now.

Calvin's travel restrictions were still in force and he cautioned me against walking the highway by myself as well, especially now that night fell by 5:00 pm, leaving little time to get to and from town on foot. Nevertheless, on December 17th I felt the need to find Mom's grave and place a memorial of some sort on it to show her spirit that I was thinking of her. I made a wreath out of some evergreen boughs and set out early in the morning, hoping to get to the hog farm before Dad woke up.

Walking through the woods, I felt a sense

of panic that I couldn't explain. I'd always felt so safe and at home in these woods and even having Spook at my side didn't calm my fears. Spook felt my tension and kept looking up at me but apparently did not sense any danger. I left him at the side of the highway as usual.

When I got to the farm, I searched all over for some sign of a newly dug grave to no avail. Just as I was about to give up, Dad came around a corner and almost bumped into me. Instead he grabbed my shoulders roughly. He smelled of decay and neglect.

"Libby," he cried, "where have you been? Why did you leave me? I've been looking for you all over!"

"Dad, it's me, Taylor. I'm not Libby. Let me go!"

A look of confusion crossed his wild eyes, then realization sank in and he let me go. "What are you doing here?" he snorted.

"I wanted to see Mom's grave and put this on it." I held the wreath up as evidence of my intentions. "Where is it? I can't find it anywhere."

More confusion clouded his bloodshot eyes. "Grave?" he repeated. "Whose grave?"

"Mom's. You said she died. Where is she?"

As the memories flooded into his consciousness, he deflated like a balloon, dropping his hands from my shoulders and slumping into the figure of an old man. Profound grief flashed across his face, and I suddenly felt sorry for him. "I'm sorry, Dad," I said. "I'm sorry I wasn't here for you."

He looked me straight in the eyes, and for a moment I saw the handsome, confident man he was when Mom fell in love with him. But it vanished just as quickly and in its place left a haggard broken man. He turned and started walking away.

"Wait. Dad! Where is Mom buried?"

He kept walking, shaking his head as he went. "Gone. My Libby's gone." His shoulders started shaking, and I realized he was sobbing.

I was shaken up by the encounter and by the mystery of Mom's missing grave. Memories of Uncle Owen's missing body and the big black hog pounded in my brain. I had to leave this place but I didn't want to go home for fear of taking bad spirits with me. So I headed for town, jogging part of the way and walking fast the rest. I made it there in just two and a half hours. On the way, the crisp clean air helped to clear my head a bit so I could figure out what to do next.

Chapter 32

Story

I instinctively went to the house shared by Ben and the guys. Ben was the only one home and he knew immediately that something was wrong. He put his arm across my shoulder and sat next to me on the couch while I told him about Mom. I was hoping someone in town would know something about her whereabouts but if so, the gossip hadn't reached Ben's ears yet. As I sniffed, trying to hold back sobs, I realized that Ben was crying silently. He looked away when I saw the tears in his eyes. I knew instinctively he wasn't crying about *my* mom.

"Tell me about her," I said gently.

It took some coaxing but he finally opened up about how he had missed seeing his mom alive by just a few days. He also told me how his dad had died in an apartment fire that burned a large portion of downtown Kansas City. I took his hands and said, "How do you cope with all the sadness, Ben? I don't even know where to start."

"Write it down, Tay," he said, using the

nickname the guys had been calling me. When I looked perplexed, he retrieved a notebook from his room upstairs and showed me pages and pages of writing, his story, he said. “You don’t have to let anyone read it. Just writing it lifts the burden on your heart.”

I nodded, thinking about Irv’s journal. While it hadn’t stopped him from ending his miserable life, maybe it had given him some relief in his last few months. I decided I needed to finish reading it to find out if it helped him.

In my mind, I saw Irv and Mom and Dad each holding up signs with words like “I hate life” and “What’s the use” and “I see ghosts” on them like in the music video *Fine Again* by Seether. Did writing down their problems help them to cope with them? Ben was adamant that it did, so I was determined to try it.

In the early afternoon as I was about to set off for home, a big group of men came into town, some on horseback or driving horse-drawn wagons, some tied together or lying prone and bloody in the back of the wagons. It looked like an after-battle scene out of a Civil War movie. Everyone wanted to know what had happened and when one of the men told us that these men were marauders who had attacked the Powell farm, my heart almost stopped, especially since none of the Powell family was among either the captors or the wounded. The man assured us that the family was okay, that their daughter-in-law had gone into labor and that's why they weren't there. I wanted to ask specifically about Calvin, but didn't want to let our secret out yet, so I hurried home to contact him by CB radio.

I got home as night was falling, and Fern was waiting for me on the porch rocking chair, a heavy blanket around her. As I told her about all that had happened, the eerie glow of another Aurora Borealis signaled yet another large CME had struck the weakened geomagnetic shield surrounding the earth.

I talked long into the night with Calvin by CB while he told me about the marauders attacking their home and about his sister-in-law's long and painful labor. He was happy to report that all were now fine, including his adorable new nephew, Joey.

After ending our talk, I got out Irv's journal and read it to the end. It was almost unbearable at times, but by the end the tone seemed to be lighter and more hopeful. He ended his journal with the following sentences: *Today I begin a new journey. Where I will go, I'm not sure, but it will not be in this world. This world holds nothing for me. I love my sister and my parents but I don't love my life.*

When I finished, I wiped my tears, took out a new notebook, and began to write my story.

Chapter 33

Reveal

Throughout the winter and the early spring, Calvin and I met every week at the guys' house in town to help them work on a top-secret project. Being the geeks we all were, we were determined to perfect a system of using Tesla coils to safely generate electricity to charge batteries for use in a wide array of appliances. The key word was 'safely' as we already knew how to make Tesla coils.

In May we felt we had perfected a system that was safely contained, and we were ready to reveal it to the people of the town and surrounding farms. We invited them to bring dead batteries of all kinds, from AAA to tractor batteries, for us to charge so that they could be used to power appliances that had not been tied to the power grid on either PF Day or PF Day 2.

The coils were built in an underground storm shelter with a thick rubber door to keep the electricity contained. We loaded the shelter with several batteries at a time, then got out, closed the door, and turned on the small battery generator that kick started the Tesla coils. After letting the batteries charge for a while, we turned off the coils and waited for the static electricity to be absorbed by the earthen walls before entering to remove the now charged batteries. Everyone was amazed at our ingenuity and we attained instant albeit short-lived celebrity status.

Calvin had invited his family to see what he had been working on in town, but he also had planned a surprise for them. That surprise had to do with me. Calvin's brother, Bracken, and his girlfriend Skylar had just gotten married and Calvin felt it was the perfect time to finally reveal our budding relationship to his family. I was understandably nervous. It's one thing to be offered a home with a family, but quite another to take their son too. Well, I didn't know if I was going to be taking him or not, but I did know that I still felt butterflies in my stomach every time I saw him. We had even begun holding hands and kissing occasionally when no one was looking.

After the Tesla demonstration, Calvin led his family and me to the patio of the guys' house and made sure we were all seated comfortably. He stood beside my chair and took my hand while I stared at the ground, my face burning with embarrassment, excitement, and anxiety. Then he spoke to his family, sounding so formal and grown up that I looked up at him to be sure it was my Calvin speaking. “Mom, Dad, and the rest of you, I have something I want to tell you.” I heard Bracken draw in his breath, and I looked over in time to see Skylar wink knowingly at him. Apparently she had known or at least guessed our secret already. “Taylor and I have been getting to know each other for a while. We want to start dating now.” He looked at me and revised his statement. “We *are* going to start dating now.” He smiled at me then we both looked at his parents. Lauren was smiling and John nodded. Whew. I was instantly relieved. Skylar and Robin, the wife of Calvin’s older brother Alex, came over to hug me while Bracken and Alex teased Calvin, punching him lightly in the arm and calling him “Romeo.”

Then Lauren, who was holding Alex and Robin’s newborn son, Joey, gave me a hug and said, “Well, I did say if there was anything you needed from us…” and we all laughed at the joke.

My once frozen and shattered heart felt very warm and almost whole that day and many of the days that followed. I guess Irv had been right—I had hope in me and I was destined for something greater than living in the shadows of addiction and neglect. But there would always be a small frozen part of my heart that wished Irv had chosen to stay alive to start a new journey together.

Chapter 34
Diamond

Not long after the revelation of our relationship, I made a decision that would impact not only my future, but also Fern's and Calvin's. I took Grammy's diamond from its sanctuary in the toe of the old lady shoe and traded it for a beautiful dappled grey horse and a small carriage. Calvin and his brothers came over to help us build a corral and a lean-to for the horse and even brought us two goats to keep it company as well as to give us milk.

After years of living on her own, only making it to town once or twice a year with Lauren, Fern was excited to be able to go to town again in the carriage. She reconnected with the few of her old friends who had survived the aftermath of the PF days and got reacquainted with some of the younger people of the town like Mrs. Littleton, who had bought her greenhouse.

I enjoyed taking her to town and showing her around, and she was happy to stay at the guys' house while we worked on our inventions. Sometimes she would even cook us meals or make us snacks in the solar oven the guys had built. The guys doted on her and called her Grandma, and she in turn spoiled them like the grandsons she never had.

Many days when we were not in town and didn't have any pressing chores at home, I'd ride the horse to Calvin's house. I enjoyed spending time with Lauren and Skylar almost as much as being with Calvin.

I've come to love that horse almost as much as Spook. The more time we spend together, the more we understand each other. I thought about all the names that would fit him—Ice, Ghost, Spirit—but in the end I decided to name him Diamond in honor of Grammy's contribution to my freedom and also the glass mere-horse, which I now realized was so much more practical and desirable than a unicorn.

Ben was right about writing my story to dull the pain of my losses. It is quite cathartic to get the ghosts out of one's mind and on to paper. It doesn't lessen the pain or remove the thoughts of lost loved ones, but it helps to make it all manageable. Although my life seems to be on a good track and Fern and I are managing survival better than most, I often find myself wishing that I could share our successes with Grammy, Irv, and Mom, and even Dad before the ghosts had eaten away his sanity.

My goal in life now as I approach the age of seventeen is to find the treasures hidden in mundane things—the new things that can be made from junk, things that were once considered worthless that now are priceless, people who were once thought of as plain but are now the real beauties—just like my broken glass unicorn and a pair of old lady shoes. Life isn't about the worth that any given society assigns something or someone, but rather the value that one can discover in everything and everyone if he or she digs deep enough.

As I breathe in the heavenly scent of the lilac bush under my window, I dream of the possibilities of our new life and what it means to survive now. And I'm filled with hope. Not just for myself, but for humanity. Maybe the devastation of PF Day will be the saving of the human race from the trap of vanity and indulgence we relished before. I hold my mere-horse up to the light streaming in my window, and I smile as the rainbow is released once again, knowing that it will always return.

If you liked Taylor's story, you might like to read Bracken's story, *How I Became a Teenage Survivalist*

Bracken soon realizes how lucky he is to live on a farm in the Midwest. What seemed like a dull and backwards life before is now the greatest chance for survival in a powerless world. Food, water, and heat are readily available, although hard work is required to make use of them. Bracken and his family must learn to survive like their ancestors who settled the land.

Or Ben's story, *Time Lost: Teenage Survivalist II*

Ben discovers that living in the middle of a big city makes survival nearly impossible. Starvation, dehydration, disease, freezing temperatures, and out-of-control fires imperil the desperate population. After facing unimaginable losses, Ben finds hope for the future when he meets Sara, who has endured her own share of agonizing loss. But when a murderous gang threatens to take away everything Ben has left, he and Sara flee to a wilderness area of a large city park where they learn to live off the land for survival.

Although each book reveals very different aspects of survival in often contrasting situations, Bracken, Ben, and Taylor prove they have what it takes to survive. Their lives eventually entwine in ways that none of them could have foreseen. The books do not have to be read in any specific order.

www.amazon.com/Julie-L.-Casey/e/B00943SWXQ

Discussion Questions

1. What were some of the themes throughout the story? How did those themes affect the story and help move it along? (Examples: ice, the unicorn/mere-horse, rainbows, ghosts, the sense of smell, etc.)

2. Why did Taylor say she had been in survival mode all her life?

3. How would you describe Taylor's personality? Is she shy, sensitive, and introverted or outgoing and gregarious? Does she confront problems head-on or try to avoid thinking about them? How does her personality type help to shape the story?

4. How smart do you think Taylor is? What clues in the story inform you about her level of intelligence?

5. What do you think about Taylor's parents? Are they bad people or good people with insurmountable mental health problems?

6. What did Grammy mean to Taylor, other than being her grandmother?

7. Why did Taylor like spiders? Why did she dislike hogs?

8. Why did Taylor refuse to eat pork from the hog farm after Uncle Owen's death? Why did she tie a towel around her face as she was frying the pork chop?

9. What were some of the personality differences between Irv and Taylor? How did it affect their relationship?

10. Why did Calvin and Taylor feel drawn to one another?

11. Why do you think Calvin and Taylor were reluctant to tell anyone besides Fern about their budding romance?

12. What do you think happened to Uncle Owen's body? How about Libby's body?

13. Why did Ben and Taylor feel an affinity toward each other? What circumstances in their lives made them understand each other's pain?

14. What do you think the future holds for Taylor?

Find Out More

"Our sun is approaching a period of high turbulence, referred to as the solar maximum, with many scientists suggesting a peak in activity around 2013." This activity could result in a coronal mass ejection which, under the perfect circumstances, could cause the collapse of the power grid as portrayed in *Ice Queen: Teenage Survivalist III.*

Find out more about solar superstorms and coronal mass ejections (CME's):

NOVA Secrets of the Sun
http://www.pbs.org/wgbh/nova/space/secrets-sun.html

The Sun's Wrath: Worst Solar Storms in History
http://www.space.com/12584-worst-solar-storms-sun-flares-history.html

NASA Science: A Super Solar Flare
http://science.nasa.gov/science-news/science-at-nasa/2008/06may_carringtonflare/

Solar Superstorm Could Knock Out US Power Grid
http://www.reuters.com/article/2012/08/04/us-solar-superstorm-idUSBRE8721K820120804

Learning how to survive without electricity is all about creative problem solving. Think about everything in your life that runs on electricity and try to figure out a way to replace each of them. The links below show how Taylor and Fern solved some of their most pressing problems.

Find out how to become a survivalist:

How to build a gravity powered light
www.youtube.com/watch?v=Q6q1oOflJT8

Top 10 Off Grid Food Preservation Methods
theprepperproject.com/top-10-off-grid-food-preservation-methods/

How to Make a Solar Powered Fan!
http://www.instructables.com/id/The-Amazing-Solar-Powered-Fan-A-Green-Gadget/

Hugelkultur
https://www.niftyhomestead.com/blog/hugelkultur/

4 Ways to Use a Cold Frame
http://www.finegardening.com/4-ways-use-cold-frame

DIY Solar Panels - Air Heaters Made of Pop Cans
http://www.instructables.com/id/Solar-panel-air-heater-made-of-pop-cans/

How to make a homemade washing machine
www.off-grid.net/2010/04/22/diy-washing-machine-and-homemade-laundry-soap/

A Message From the Author:

Thank you for taking the time to read my book. I would be honored if you would consider leaving a review for it on ***Amazon***.

I'd like to shout a big thank you to all my family, friends, and fantastic supporters of the Teenage Survivalist series.
You all are the best!

About the Author

Julie Casey lives in a rural area near St. Joseph, Missouri, with her husband, Jonn Casey, a science teacher, and their three youngest sons. After teaching preschool for fifteen years, she has been homeschooling her four sons for ten years. Julie has Bachelor of Science degrees in education and computer programming and has written four books. She enjoys historical reenacting, wildlife rehabilitation, teaching her children, and writing books that capture the imaginations of young people.

Find out more at www.julielcasey.com.

Check out these other titles from

Julie L. Casey

How I Became a Teenage Survivalist

Time Lost: Teenage Survivalist II

Defenders of Holt

Stop Beating the Dead Horse

In Daddy's Hands

Check out these Middle Grade and Young Adult Books from

Amazing Things Press

How I Became a Teenage Survivalist by Julie L. Casey

Time Lost: Teenage Survivalist II by Julie L. Casey

Convolutions by Vashti Daise

Nikki's Heart by Nona j. Moss

I, Eugenius by Larry W. Anderson

Defenders of Holt by Julie L. Casey

A Thin Strip of Green by Vashti Daise

Trade of the Tricks: The Tricks' Brand by David Noe

I Am Currency by Whitney L. Grady

Pass of the Crow by Whitney L. Grady

Owners of the Sky by Whitney L. Grady

Tales of an Alien Invader 2: Camp Orion by Michelle Brown

Entwined Courage by Tracy Lane

John Henry's War by Larry W. Anderson

Amazing Things Press

www.amazingthingspress.com

52064955R00096

Made in the USA
San Bernardino, CA
09 August 2017